What people are saying about THE ROSE TATTOO:

UNLAWFULLY WEDDED
"Extremely well-done."
— *Rendezvous*

UNDYING LAUGHTER
"Kelsey Roberts displays a glorious sense of humor in UNDYING LAUGHTER...."
— Debbie Richardson, *Romantic Times*

HANDSOME AS SIN
"Kelsey Roberts once again delivers sparkling dialogue and great touches of humor."
— Debbie Richardson, *Romantic Times*

THE TALL, DARK ALIBI
"The plot is exciting, the hero dangerous, and the chemistry! It was so good I hated to reach the last page."
— Laurel Gainer, *Affaire de Coeur*

THE SILENT GROOM
"Kelsey Roberts will take you on a fun, fanciful and fascinating journey.... If you are looking for romance and intrigue with a twist, you won't want to miss her."
— Nora Roberts

THE WRONG MAN
"Roberts employs a masterful talent for hooking the reader with incredible suspense..."
— *Gothic Journal*

HER MOTHER'S ARMS
"Talented Kelsey Roberts masterfully blends the old and the new in HER MOTHER'S ARMS."
— Debbie Richardson, *Romantic Times*

UNFORGETTABLE NIGHT
"This story...an intriguing mix of suspense, passion, humor and warmth...will keep you hooked..."
— *Rendezvous*

Dear Reader,

People get wanderlust, and imaginary ones are no different. So you'll find this book a little different from the others in this series. Once again, Rose Porter acts as the catalyst for another story. When Rose is asked to put together a private party for Barbara Prather, she does it in usual Rose fashion. With the waiters dressed as Elvis, can this be anything but a unique affair?

Barbara's life is turned upside down after the party, and her only link to solid ground is Cade Landry. He's self-assured and knows what he wants. And he wants Barbara. He's a rancher from the wilds of Montana, which doesn't exactly suit Barbara's metropolitan style. Together they work through a maze of secrets, blackmail, deception and a murderous Elvis.

This book introduces you to the Landry family from Jasper, Montana. Beginning in October, please watch for the launch of my new series about seven of Montana's most eligible brothers. I'm really excited to be given the opportunity to go west for a little while. I'll still be visiting the Rose Tattoo since I have to find true love for Susan. I'd love to know what you think! Please write to me c/o Harlequin Books, 300 East 42nd Street, 6th Floor, New York, New York 10017 and don't forget to visit Harlequin on the web at www.romance.net.

Happy Reading!

Kelsey Roberts

Kelsey Roberts

Wanted: Cowboy

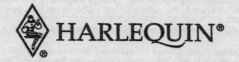

HARLEQUIN®

TORONTO • NEW YORK • LONDON
AMSTERDAM • PARIS • SYDNEY • HAMBURG
STOCKHOLM • ATHENS • TOKYO • MILAN • MADRID
PRAGUE • WARSAW • BUDAPEST • AUCKLAND

In loving memory of my uncle,
Robert Hampton Hale (1924-1998)

ISBN 0-373-22522-9

WANTED: COWBOY

Visit us at www.romance.net

Printed in U.S.A.

Drawing by Linda Harding Shaw

CAST OF CHARACTERS

Barbara Prather—Her special party became a funeral—and she was next on Elvis's hit list.

Cade Landry—Protecting the city slicker suddenly seemed less hazardous than falling for her charms....

Dale Breck—The dead man would be truly missed—or would he?

Harriet Hilton—Grieving widow or crafty blackmailer?

Jessica Landry—Cade's daughter wanted her daddy all to herself.

Olivia Miles—Her talent and organization saved Barbara's project. Was she too good to be true?

Rose Porter—The eccentric owner of the Rose Tattoo always added extra spice to her events....

Thomas Shelton—Barbara's business rival had the annoying habit of turning up at the most inconvenient times.

Elvis—He'd chosen the perfect disguise—but the hit wasn't *quite* perfect....

Prologue

"Is everything all set?"

"To the last detail."

"Are you sure?"

"Quit worrying. I'm on top of things."

"I don't know why you can't do this yourself. You aren't exactly the most ethical person I've ever encountered."

"I don't remember you complaining when you took the money."

"Money was one thing. This is different."

"This will make us rich."

"If we don't get caught."

"We won't. But we *will* be rich."

They shared a laugh in the moonless darkness of the secluded park.

"What about Landry? Will he be a problem?"

"No."

"Who else will be there?"

"All eight members of the board and some guests of the Prather woman. How are you going to do it?"

"The less you know the better. Suffice to say it wouldn't be prudent for me to do this alone. The few people who know are—"

"What! How many people are involved? More people means more opportunity for someone to point the finger at us."

"Quiet! There's no way anyone will ever connect us. It isn't like I can pull the trigger myself. I had no choice but to hire a professional."

"We're going to get caught."

"Not if you keep your cool and do exactly what I said. Everything else has been arranged."

"When do I get my money?"

"In a hurry?" A humorless laugh accompanied the question.

"I wouldn't be doing this otherwise. I need the cash as soon as possible."

"And you'll get it."

"When?"

"When the target is eliminated."

Chapter One

"We won't be using her."

Cade Landry raked his hands through his hair in frustration. "Then explain to me why I just spent seven hours flying us here."

Dale chuckled. The action rumbled from deep within the large man's out-of-shape midsection. He placed his hand on Cade's shoulder and said, "Stop complaining, son. The Prather woman is sure to make the evening worth our while."

Sighing, Cade turned to look out the one-way glass of the limo's window. "We can have a nice dinner in Jasper. We didn't need to waste a whole day and night coming to Charleston."

"I hear she's a looker," Dale said, as if that somehow explained everything. "I know how you appreciate a pretty girl."

"I can find a pretty woman in Montana," Cade argued. "I've got work on top of work at my spread."

Again Dale chuckled. "And it'll be waiting for you in the morning. Loosen up, son. This little soiree is part and parcel of the cartel's business. As vice president, you have a duty to attend these things.''

''*You* have a duty,'' Cade said. ''The other members will go with whatever firm you recommend.''

Dale gave him a gentle shove. ''Relax and enjoy yourself. This is one of the perks of the job.''

''Not if you have no intention of using Prather and Associates for the ad campaign.''

''We can't let a woman handle our advertising,'' Dale said with a dismissive wave of his large hand. ''But we *can* let her throw us a party and pitch her ideas.''

''This isn't like you, Dale,'' Cade commented. ''If you aren't going to consider her work, why bother coming all this way?''

Dale's smile didn't reach his eyes. ''I'll consider her work. I just don't have any intention of hiring her.''

''So what am I supposed to do?''

''Relax, enjoy some Southern hospitality. I'm sure Miss Prather has gone all out to impress us.''

Cade blew out a breath and pushed himself against the soft upholstery, resigned in the knowledge that the evening would most likely be a total waste of his time.

''PLEASE TELL ME this is a joke!'' Barbara cried as she peered in through the glass doors.

''What do you mean a *joke?*'' Rose Porter asked

defensively. "I worked my butt off to make it special for you."

"Special?" Barbara parroted. "I asked for a themed cocktail reception for cattlemen, Rose. Not a tribute to The King."

"Tribute" is putting it mildly, Barbara thought as she adjusted the straps of her simple black dress. The second-floor banquet room of the Rose Tattoo's recent expansion had been turned into a replica of Elvis's home, Graceland. She counted thirteen waiters dressed as the young Elvis and three waitresses—including her friend, Susan—dressed as Priscilla during her jet-black-hair phase.

Barbara closed her eyes for a moment, relatively sure her dream of taking Prather and Associates advertising agency national was circling the drain.

"I don't know why you're in such a snit," Rose complained. "We worked hard getting this just right." The co-owner of the restaurant patted her temporarily colored, well-lacquered hair.

She was dressed as Elvis's mother, Gladys Presley. In a strange way, Barbara found the getup less bizarre than Rose's usual fashions. Rose's taste in clothing and accessories included lots of Lycra and loud animal prints. It was the first time in years Barbara had seen her without gaudy plastic earrings and bleached-blond hair.

"Rose, I was thinking more along the lines of a Western theme. I wanted to make the board of the Cattlemen's Cartel feel at home."

Rose stiffened, clearly hurt. "Then you should've returned some of my phone calls. With Shelby still out with the new baby, I tried to get your input. All you ever said was 'Do whatever.'"

That was true. Running her hand through her hair, Barbara let out a long sigh. She'd been too busy preparing her presentation. She hadn't had time to oversee the details for the reception since there were no associates at Prather and Associates. Though she had a secretary and sometimes hired temps, it was still a one-woman operation. Landing the cattlemen's account would have meant going national.

Looking at Rose, Barbara gave a small smile as she said, "I'm sorry. You're right. I did tell you to do whatever you wanted." *Which was incredibly stupid,* she added silently.

Her apology appeared to placate Rose. Her bright red lips curved into a wide smile. "Aren't the waiters wonderful?"

"Where did you find them?" Barbara asked.

"I called a local talent agency on East Bay. They put me in touch with some struggling local actors. *Unemployed* local actors, who actually have more experience waiting tables than acting," Rose said with a laugh.

Barbara checked her watch. "I guess I should go take my place at the front door."

"You go on. They'll love it," Rose insisted. "Everyone loves Elvis."

"Let's hope so," she grumbled under her breath.

"Love Me Tender" was playing as Barbara walked from the porch into the wilds of the banquet room. Susan Taylor waved and rushed over. "What do you think?" she asked, motioning in an arc with her arm. "I wanted to replicate Elvis's living room, but Rose insisted we recreate his jungle room instead."

"I wish you'd have warned me," Barbara said after making sure Rose wasn't within earshot.

Susan reached out and gave her a one-armed hug. "Warned you? You've been unavailable for weeks."

"I've been trying to stay one step ahead of Thomas Shelton's firm. I swear the guy popped up out of nowhere. I've never even heard of him, but he's definitely been busy making sure Dale Breck has."

"Have some faith in your talent," Susan said. "I think this whole party idea is wonderful and I'm sure all those cowboys will be impressed. Who knows, you might even meet a new man."

"Let's hope they like it," Barbara murmured. Fixing her eyes on Susan, she added, "And I don't need to meet new men. I meet men."

Susan's darkened eyebrows pulled together as she frowned. "Right, you meet a lot of men. When?"

Barbara shrugged. "At the grocery store."

Susan scowled. "Men in aprons watering produce every fifteen minutes doesn't count as meeting new men."

"Works for me. Besides, I don't have time for men right now."

"Oh, lighten up, Barbara. I'm sensing a lot of negative energy from you. It's totally spoiling the karma in this room."

"I think the deep-fried peanut butter and mashed banana canapés are the problem, not my energy."

"That sandwich was Elvis's favorite food," Susan explained. "Besides, we've got a ton of other stuff to serve. The peanut butter things were just to add to the ambiance."

Knowing there was nothing she could do in only five minutes, Barbara turned her attention to other things. "Do I look all right?"

"Sure," Susan said. "Though your little black dress is a tad on the conservative side. Don't you know that red is a power color? You should've worn red. And according to my aromatherapist, a dab of vanilla at the wrist is both soothing and—"

"Thanks," Barbara interrupted. As much as she loved Susan, she wasn't in the mood to listen to her most recent New Age endeavor. "I've got to get downstairs."

At precisely seven, the first car arrived at the Rose Tattoo. Barbara took two deep breaths and plastered a smile on her face as an older, distinguished gentleman stepped from the car clasping a Stetson.

"You must be Miss Prather," he said as he extended his hand. "Dale Breck, ma'am."

"Welcome to Charleston, Mr. Breck."

He smiled as he withdrew his beefy hand. "Call me Dale, honey. Thanks for the invite. It isn't every day that I have an opportunity to have dinner with a pretty thing like you.''

Barbara swallowed an acerbic retort at being called both ''honey'' and a ''pretty thing.'' ''I'm glad you accepted my invitation.''

''I never turn down a free meal with a pretty girl,'' Dale said with a belly laugh.

Given the girth of his belly, the sound was almost as loud as his voice. *Pretty girl?* Barbara thought. *The man is a bigger sexist pig in person!* When her smile threatened to slip, she tacked it back into place. She reminded herself that she wanted this account. Unfortunately, she also longed to give Dale Breck a lesson from Feminism 101, with a little professional etiquette thrown in for good measure.

''I've got to tell you, gal, bringing us all here to Charleston for dinner is impressive. It sure is a change from the way Mr. Shelton does business.''

Barbara longed to ask just exactly what Mr. Shelton was doing to woo the cartel, but she knew better. If she opened her mouth, Breck was sure to think she was worried by the competition. Which, of course, she was.

''Hurry on up!'' Dale called over his shoulder. ''Come see our hostess, Cade. She'll put some life into your step.''

Barbara was silently counting to ten when the man stepped from the car. She believed nothing could have usurped her growing anger at the sexist way Dale was speaking to her and the knowledge that Shelton was nipping at her heels.

She was wrong.

"This here is Cade Landry." Dale half shoved him in her direction. Adding a slap to the man's back, he said, "He's like a son to me."

He's like a dream to me! No, make that a god, she amended as she took in the broad shoulders, tapered waist and powerful thighs. The man had an incredible body, but that wasn't what lighted the fire in the pit of her stomach. It was his intense, hypnotic, gray-green eyes peering down at her.

"Hello, Miss Prather," he said, extending his hand.

"M-Mr. Landry."

His hand was warm and strong. Barbara had an overwhelming urge to yank him to her right there in the middle of the sidewalk. *Now who needs a lecture on professional etiquette?*

"Cade."

The single word, spoken in a deep, rich voice, was an effective complement to more than six feet of rugged, masculine perfection. Barbara was glad she had on heels, otherwise her toes would have curled as he slowly released her hand.

"Cade," she managed in a more appropriate voice. "Welcome to Charleston."

Reluctantly, Barbara turned her attention to greeting the other eight men who had come to Charleston at her expense. She'd spent an outrageous amount of money but hoped it would prove a wise investment.

Not to mention the added benefit of outdoing anything Shelton might have in mind.

Holding her breath, she led her small contingent inside the restaurant. *Do I warn them?*

Her arm was looped through Dale's as they moved toward the horse-shaped bar. Dale grasped her fingers and stopped abruptly. "I'll be damned," he exclaimed. He dropped Barbara's arm and stepped forward to shake the hand of a man at the bar. "I didn't expect you to be here," he said. Barbara noted genuine surprise on the older man's face. Dale glanced at her and gave a wink. "You must be pretty sure of yourself to be comfortable enough to do this."

Barbara smiled as she studied the man shaking Dale's hand. He looked about twenty-five. He had hair that was almost as brilliant a red as her own, but that was the only thing familiar about the mystery man.

"I'm sorry," she managed through her tight smile, "I'll take credit for anything that impresses you Mr. Breck, but having a friend of yours here in the bar wasn't my doing."

Hearing a faint, masculine chuckle, she glanced back at Cade Landry. His eyes were positively dancing with amusement. Dipping his head forward as he stepped closer, his breath teased her ear. "Where I come from, we call this an ambush."

"W-what?" she asked as she moved away from him.

Cade's smile broadened. "Er, Dale...I believe Miss Prather needs an introduction."

Dale shrugged as if confused. "You mean you didn't invite Thomas here?"

Barbara felt her eyes widen as she turned her attention to the red-haired man. "You're Thomas Shelton?"

His smile dripped charm. "Why, Miss Prather, this is a coincidence."

She took the hand he offered and shook it while she fantasized about wrapping the same hand around the man's throat. "Coincidence?" *My butt,* she added. "I thought your office was in New York."

His gracious expression didn't falter. "It is. I'm here in Charleston on vacation."

"On the same night I'm entertaining Mr. Breck and his associates?" she asked with an equal measure of civility.

"As I said," he sighed, "an amazing coincidence." Shelton looked at his watch. "But a brief one. I'm meeting a friend, so I'll have to be going."

Thank God. "What a shame." Slipping her hand around Breck's arm, she said, "We wouldn't want to keep you. Gentlemen, please come with me."

"Nice to meet you!" Shelton called to her back.

"Same here," she said as she led the men toward the porch stairs.

"I'll be damned again," Dale said with a laugh when they reached the banquet room. "If this isn't a treat. Honey,'' he began as he placed a hand on her shoulder, "how did you know I was an Elvis fan?''

Barbara shrugged, hoping to dislodge his hand. It didn't work. "Isn't everyone?''

A faux Elvis came over with a tray of champagne glasses. The other hired Elvises took bar orders or carried trays full of various offerings.

Barbara began to relax after about twenty minutes when it appeared that all the cattlemen were enjoying themselves. She was silently fuming at Shelton. *The backstabbing, lying SOB.* She took a champagne flute from a passing Elvis and stepped out onto the second-story porch for a breath of fresh air and to silently practice her pitch for the account one more time.

"Don't Be Cruel'' was playing and she prayed that wasn't an omen of things to come. *Lord, I'm starting to sound like Susan!* she berated herself as she went to the railing, sipped her drink and concentrated on media buys and storyboards.

"I don't like Elvis,'' Cade Landry said.

With her back turned, Barbara was startled by his sudden appearance on the deserted porch. She actually jumped, spilling a decent amount of her drink. "Blast!'' she muttered as she shook champagne from one hand and wiped at the front of her dress with the other.

"Sorry,'' he said as he reached over her shoulder and handed her a cocktail napkin.

Barbara put her glass on the railing as she grabbed the napkin from him. "No problem.''

"I didn't mean to scare you."

"Then you shouldn't sneak up behind people." She turned and found him looking down at her with amusement in his piercing gaze. "Is something funny, Mr. Landry? I'm glad my spilling champagne on a classic Versace has entertained you. That should more than make up for the Elvis thing."

The amusement didn't leave his eyes. In fact, it spread to his mouth as his lips curved into a very lopsided, very sexy smile. "Don't forget how much fun I had watching you restrain yourself downstairs. That was impressive."

"I'm so glad the evening is working for you."

Cade's grin remained in place. "I thought you did a fair job handling Shelton's surprise appearance."

She blotted at the dampness. "I'd love to know how he learned about the party."

Cade shrugged his broad shoulders. "I might have mentioned it."

She glared at him. "Thanks a lot. Do you have any idea what this party is costing me? Not to mention the expense of flying eight of you here."

Cade appeared totally unrepentant. "*I* flew us here," he reminded her. Cade was standing close to her. His large body blocked her vision. Had it not been for the sounds of laughter and muffled conversation in the background, it would have seemed as if they were the only two people in Charleston. When she met his eyes, she again felt that urge to do more than say hello. She must be losing her grip. He'd just confessed to plotting against her, and all she could do was fantasize about what it might be like to be held against that incredible body.

The man was just too perfect. Cade Landry was like no man she had ever encountered. She was used to the stockbroker type—perfectly capped teeth, manicured hands and thousand-dollar suits. Cade wore faded jeans and an off-the-rack chocolate-brown jacket that almost exactly matched the color of his hair. His hair fell to his shoulders—a style that usually turned her right off—but it suited his rugged persona. He looked a lot like an updated version of the Marlboro Man, minus the cigarette.

He took a step closer. "May I offer to pay for the cleaning?"

"Not necessary," she sighed.

"That's right," he drawled. "Dale said you were rich."

"Did he?" She could smell his subtle, woodsy cologne.

"He didn't tell me you were beautiful."

Beautiful? Try not to swoon! Very unprofessional! "I suppose that's because Dale and I have never met personally. We've been talking on the phone, mostly."

"If you're rich and beautiful, how come you're working so hard to handle our advertising?"

His question was a rush of cold water that doused her silent musings. With a saccharine voice, she replied, "I had some spare time between charity tennis events and debutante balls."

"Testy little thing, aren't you?" he chortled.

She glared up at him. "I am not a 'little thing.' I'm a grown woman, Mr. Landry."

Leaning closer, he said, "I noticed."

Her temper was reaching critical mass, so she reminded herself that Dale Breck thought of this man as a son. A son who, in her opinion, could benefit from some sensitivity training. "I hope you also noticed that I've invited several of my current clients here this evening. Please feel free to speak to them regarding my handling of their advertising."

Cade took another step closer, so that his handsome face loomed just above her. In a voice as deep and smooth as imported dark chocolates, he whispered, "I'm right interested in learning how you handle things."

"I've got to get back inside," she said as she started to duck past him. She didn't get very far. He touched his fingers to her bare arm.

"No need to rush off."

Barbara was about to insist when Dale stepped out onto the porch. He was smiling as if catching her on the porch with Cade was his only reason for being in Charleston.

"I knew I could count on you," Dale said with a slap and a rather vulgar wink to Cade. "He's a fast worker with the girls."

Barbara tried to smile, but it was impossible. "I don't recall inviting any girls."

Dale's lecherous grin faltered for a second as he took a slight side step out of the doorway leading to the banquet room. Barbara noticed Cade hiding a grin as he excused himself and moved away to join the crowd inside.

An Elvis came toward Barbara and Dale, his tray covered with champagne-filled glasses. Barbara hoped to use his arrival as a diversion. She shouldn't have snapped at Dale. Definitely not good for business. If she wanted the account, she needed to rein in her genuine dislike for the man and his pseudo son.

Just as the Elvis stepped onto the porch, she reached for Dale to turn him around and steer him to the waiter. When the Elvis reached into the sleeve of his shirt, she expected him to offer them napkins. Instead, he produced a gun, and before she could react, he fired.

Chapter Two

Cade sat alone at a table in the bar of the Rose Tattoo. Toying with a stir stick, he glanced around the room as the reality that Dale was dead set in.

In the hours since the shooting, he'd been trying to make sense of it. That was proving impossible. *Why would a hired Elvis kill Dale? And why here in Charleston?*

A waitress approached him. "Is there anything I can get you?" she asked.

"Whiskey. Neat."

She nodded, then went back to the horseshoe-shaped bar and poured the drink herself. It wasn't as if she had any options. The police had questioned and released all the regular patrons. Now they were down to the members of the cartel and the wait staff for the party.

And Barbara Prather. Just saying her name in his head brought a vivid image to mind. He would go to his grave remembering the horrified look in her blue eyes when Dale's lifeless body fell on top of her. The rest of those frantic moments following the shooting was little more than a blur.

"Would you like something else?" the waitress inquired as she slid the highball glass onto the table. "I'd be happy to get you something to eat."

He shook his head. "Thanks, but the only thing I'd like to do now is get out of here."

"I sense your pain," she said as she leaned against the back of the chair opposite his own. "I'm Susan."

Cade took a long swallow of the burning liquid. "Well, Susan, any idea how long they plan to keep us here?"

"They have to interview everyone," she explained. "I offered to call Miss Zinnia, but Dalton and his partner weren't interested. I know she could help."

"Miss Zinnia?" Cade prompted.

The waitress's eyes, which were tinted violet by contact lenses, grew larger and her expression became animated. "She's my psychic. She has a real gift. She can see things the rest of us can't."

Yeah, right, Cade thought. "Right now, I'd like to see the inside of my plane," Cade grumbled. "I need to get back to make arrangements for Mr. Breck."

"Barbara can see to that," Susan insisted.

"Barbara?"

She nodded vigorously, which caused some of her teased, dyed-black hair to work free. "I know she feels responsible. I'm sure she'll take care of everything. She's really good at planning."

Completely disgusted and very angry, Cade

glanced around at the Elvises and Priscillas. "I don't think so. I'm afraid she'd re-create The King's last day as an encore."

"No!" Susan wailed. "This wasn't Barbara's idea."

"It was her party." Cade took another swallow.

A uniformed officer appeared and told Cade he was to go up to the offices for his interview. He followed the policeman into the kitchen, where apparently everything had stopped at the time of the shooting. Plates of food beneath the heat lamps had long since dried out, and in one area, a carrot was abandoned half-chopped.

A narrow, creaking staircase took him to the second floor. Unlike the banquet room in the addition, this space was old and cluttered. It looked more like the second floor of a home than the offices of a business.

Cade was ushered into a room at the end of the hall. There he found Barbara, the woman dressed as Gladys Presley and two men in suits.

The taller, dark-haired one stepped forward and extended his hand, then said, "I'm Detective Dalton Ross and this is my partner, Detective Jackson."

Cade acknowledged the men with a single dip of his head. "Who are you?" he asked the Gladys woman.

"Rose Porter. I own this place."

At that moment, he had the impression that Rose was sorry she was the proprietor. "Why are you here?'' he asked Barbara. ''I thought police questioning was done in private.''

''Miss Prather is a friend of mine,'' Detective Ross said. ''I can vouch for her.''

''Really?'' Cade lashed out. ''Then where the hell were you when she was arranging this murder?''

''What?'' Barbara fairly screamed as she sprang to her feet. ''How dare you?''

He took a step to stand directly in front of her. It was an attempt to intimidate her. It didn't work. He glared down at her upturned face. ''I *dare* because you arranged all this.''

''Mr. Landry,'' the blond one—Jackson—said as he placed a hand on Cade's shoulder, ''I know you're upset, but we really need to ask you some questions.''

Reluctantly, Cade turned away from the redhead and gave his attention to the two detectives. He wasn't willing to totally cooperate, so he didn't take the seat offered him.

Detective Ross opened a small notepad and asked, ''Do you know of anyone with a reason to kill Mr. Breck?''

''Nope.''

''Did he mention getting any threats? Or any other contact he felt was strange?''

''Nope.''

Ross appeared nonplussed as he thumbed through some of the pages in his hand. ''Let's back up. What did Mr. Breck do for the cartel?''

''He is—was—the president.''

"What is the purpose of the cartel?"

Cade shrugged. "We're a group of Montana cattlemen. We pool our resources for advertising and public education. Didn't the others explain all this to you?"

"Yes," Ross answered. "Please understand that it's our job to question everyone thoroughly. The rest of your associates have provided statements and Barbara has made arrangements for them at the Omni for the night."

"Nice touch," he said, glowering at the defiant woman. "Is a five-star hotel supposed to make us forget that our friend was murdered at your party?"

She didn't back down even a fraction of an inch. "No. I just wanted to make everyone as comfortable as possible after such a tragedy."

"Can we get back on track?" the detective asked. "What does the cartel do?"

Cade rubbed his hands over his face and let out a breath. "We advertise to entice people to buy beef. We also produce educational pamphlets to dispel the myth that eating beef is a ticket to a heart attack."

"Does the cartel ever get threats from other organizations?"

Cade gave a mirthless laugh. "The usual. The radical vegetarian groups and the animal rights people don't usually send us Christmas cards."

Ross seemed to see possibilities in his response. "Have any of these groups sent anything recently?

Or publicly criticized the organization or Mr. Breck individually?''

"They usually target the slaughterhouses, not the ranchers," Cade explained. "On any given day, a handful of protesters are picketing. Only once, during all that mad cow fuss, have they ever picketed the cartel office in Helena.''

"Was Mr. Breck the president then?''

Cade nodded. "He's been our only president.''

"How did he react?''

"He didn't," Cade assured him. "We're beef producers, Detective, not political activists. All we want is a fair price for our cattle. Having a bunch of people with nothing better to do than walk up and down a sidewalk in the summer heat or a winter blizzard wasn't ever an issue for any of us. They have every right to voice their opinions.''

Jackson then asked, "You don't recall if any of the protesters had a voice that was louder than the others?''

"Nope. Like I said, none of us took it personally. Including Dale.''

"Marital problems or other personal problems?'' Ross asked.

Cade shook his head. "Dale's wife died more than a decade ago. No kids. Speaking of which, I really need to use the phone. I don't want my daughter to hear on the news that a cattleman was murdered by a psychotic Elvis.''

The detectives huddled with Barbara and Rose

while he phoned the Lazy L and spoke first to his housekeeper, Mrs. Granger, then to his daughter, Jessica. It was annoying that he wasn't shown the simple courtesy of having a private conversation. He was forced to spend several minutes comforting his daughter after telling her that Dale was dead.

When he was finished, he felt drained. Maybe it was some sort of delayed reaction to the murder. The cause didn't matter; he was beat.

"How much longer is this going to take?" he asked, knowing full well he wasn't going home. He was in no shape to fly and he needed to arrange to have Dale's body flown back to Montana.

"We can finish this in the morning," Ross suggested after a silent communication with his partner. "We still have to speak with all twelve of the Elvises."

"Twelve?" he heard Barbara exclaim.

"You mean eleven," Rose interjected. "I hired twelve. The one who fired the shots ran out through the back."

The detective again conferred with his notepad. "The uniforms took twelve names," he said. "Hey, Brigham!" he called, summoning the same young officer who'd escorted Cade to the office. "Go downstairs and count the Elvises."

"Excuse me?" the officer said, his lips quivering as he apparently battled the urge to smile.

"You heard the detective," Jackson barked. "Go down and count the Elvises."

In the five minutes it took for Brigham to do a recount, Cade explained the cartel in more detail. ''There has to be some other explanation,'' he told the detectives. ''No one associated with the cartel had any reason to kill Dale.''

''There was no dissention among the members?'' Jackson asked.

''Sure,'' Cade admitted. ''But no more so than on the board of any other organization.''

''How much did Mr. Breck earn for acting as president?''

''Twenty grand a year, plus expenses for travel and reimbursement for phone calls and other things he did from home.''

''Why would he do things from home? I thought you said the cartel had an office,'' Ross said.

Cade offered a slight sneer. ''Montana is a big place, Detective. Yes, the cartel kept an office in Helena, but Dale's spread was more than seventy miles northwest. It wouldn't make sense to expect him to drive all that way to make a phone call, now would it?''

Cade turned in the direction of approaching footsteps. Brigham returned and verified that there were currently a dozen Elvises in the Rose Tattoo's bar.

''That isn't possible,'' Rose insisted. ''I only hired twelve.''

''That makes sense,'' Barbara said. ''I thought I counted thirteen.''

"Why didn't you say so before?" Ross challenged her.

Barbara gave him a withering stare. "I didn't know there was any discrepancy in the number."

The detectives exchanged glances. Then Ross spoke. "Okay, who knew of your plans for the party?"

Barbara appeared to defer to the owner, then said, "Lots of people, I guess. I wasn't exactly making a secret of it."

"I used an agency to hire the Elvises, so I have no idea who would've known," Rose said defensively.

"We know one thing for sure," Jackson said.

"Yeah, we know Dale is dead," Cade retorted.

"Yes," the detective conceded. "This was obviously a well-planned hit."

"That just doesn't make any sense," Cade argued. "Dale didn't have an enemy."

"That you know of," Ross countered. "It also means you're in trouble, Barbara."

"I didn't do anything!" Barbara insisted.

"Not that kind of trouble," Ross amended. "I was alluding to the fact that you are the only witness to the shooting, and you can identify the killer."

Cade rolled his eyes. "Right. She can swear it was the young Elvis."

"I can't identify anyone," Barbara objected. "He's got to know that."

"Maybe," Ross hedged. "But until we have more, I think you should go to a safe house."

"A safe house?" Barbara repeated.

"We can protect you that way."

"Forget it, Dalton," Barbara said. "I'm not going to let you scare me into hiding. Find Elvis and put *him* in a safe house. And while you're at it, find a guy named Thomas Shelton."

"Shelton?" Rose asked as he wrote the name in his notepad.

"He's been after the cartel account. He lives and works in New York, but he was here at the bar less than an hour before the shooting."

Cade met her heated blue eyes. "Shelton wanted to do business with us. Why would he kill Dale?"

Her expression grew even angrier. "News flash, cowboy. I wanted the account, too. I had no reason to kill the man who was going to give it to me."

Cade felt his own anger simmering. "He wasn't going to give you the account."

"I didn't even have an opportunity to make my presentation, so you don't know what you're talking about," Barbara argued.

Cade shrugged. "Trust me, it wouldn't have made any difference. Dale wouldn't have hired you, and you must have figured that out and decided to have him killed."

"Right," Barbara seethed as she glared at him with furious eyes. "I make a habit of killing people who don't hire me. I'll assume you've been kicked in the head once too often, Mr. Landry. Since the alternative is to publicly acknowledge the fact that you're an idiot.''

''Uh,'' Ross interrupted, ''can we get back to the issue of your safety?''

''I am safe, Dalton,'' Barbara insisted. ''I have a condo with perfectly good locks and a security system.''

''C'mon, Barbara,'' Ross pleaded. ''Haley will have a fit if I don't protect you. I already blew it with Claire.''

Cade saw a flicker of sadness in Barbara's eyes at the mention of the name. ''Who's Claire?''

''She was murdered,'' Barbara responded evasively.

Ross cleared his throat and added, ''Claire was a friend of my wife's and Barbara's. She was murdered a couple of years ago. Barbara was held hostage by the killer.''

''Let's not go into that,'' Barbara said. ''Not when Mr. Landry has already branded *me* a killer.''

''Please do as I ask,'' Ross said determinedly.

Surprising even himself, Cade said, ''She can come home with me.''

Barbara blinked, her expression frozen as she appeared to consider his spur-of-the-moment suggestion. ''Let me get this straight,'' she said. ''You accused me of arranging the murder no more than a minute ago. Now you're suggesting that I go home with you?'' Her eyes narrowed as she spoke. ''How much sense does that make? Dale was from Montana.

You live in Montana. What makes you think I'd be safe in Montana?''

"Because the Lazy L is secluded and I have hands who guard the airstrip and ride the fences. No one gets in or out without my knowing about it.''

"Consider the safe house, Barbara, please?'' Ross asked.

"I did and the answer is still no. And I'm not going off to some dusty ranch to hide from Elvis. The whole idea is stupid.''

"Suit yourself,'' Cade said.

"Barbara,'' Rose began, "please go where it's safe. Dalton is right. You need to get away from here.''

"I don't want to go someplace where I'm being watched twenty-four hours a day. And I sure don't want to go with him. What would I do on a ranch?'' Barbara asked.

"You can pitch your ideas for our account,'' Cade supplied.

"To whom? The cattle?''

"To me,'' he said on a sigh. "I'm the vice president of the Cattlemen's Cartel, which means I'm the one you have to convince now.''

Chapter Three

"You have to leave."

"Be reasonable, Barbara," Dalton argued. "I'll sack out on the couch and—"

"You will not," she cut in as she took his arm and led him to the door. "Go home to your wife. Elvis has got to know I couldn't identify him and I've got locks and an alarm. This place is totally safe."

"No place is totally safe," the detective insisted. "Come home with me. Haley will—"

"Worry needlessly," Barbara finished for him. "I'm not worried, Dalton. Promise." She crossed her heart.

"I'm going to have a patrol unit come by regularly."

"Fine," Barbara said as she opened the door and gave him a second shove. "Go home."

Dalton let out a breath and she saw the indecision on his face.

"This isn't smart, Barbara. My gut tells me you need protection."

She reached up and patted his cheek. "Your gut is being an overprotective friend whom I love, but I really do want to be alone right now."

"No wonder you and Haley are friends. You share a stubborn streak," he groused as he bent and kissed her cheek. "I want you to call in the morning. I'll send a car to follow you to work."

"Go home, Dalton!" she called as she shut the door, locked the bolt and slipped the chain into place.

She peeled off her bloodstained dress as she reached the second floor. Balling it up, she tossed it into the trash. Versace or not, she knew she'd never be able to wear it again without reliving the horror of the shooting.

Shivering at the memory, Barbara slipped into the shower and turned the water on full blast. Her skin tingled almost painfully as she scrubbed herself with the sea sponge. She'd hoped a shower would wash away the memories. It didn't, but the hot water relaxed her a little.

Leaving her hair wrapped in a towel, she pulled on her black silk robe and went downstairs. The house was quiet. Too quiet, she decided. She stopped in the living room, put a CD in the stereo and pressed the play button. An up-tempo Latin beat filled the house as she went from room to room, turning on lights.

"I'm being silly," she whispered to herself as she

headed to the refrigerator and pulled a bottle of Chardonnay from the sparse contents.

Her gaze veered to the alarm keypad by the double glass doors. Seeing the red "armed" button flash gave her a sense of security as she poured herself a drink. Taking her glass and the bottle, she returned to the second floor, but not before checking all the locks as well as the alarm keypad by the front door.

While she sat on the edge of her bed, she pulled off the towel and absently used it to dry her hair. The CD was playing the next to last song as she locked her bedroom door, refilled her glass and willed herself not to think about Dale Breck's expression as the bullet ripped through him.

"Think of something else," she chided as she took the towel to the adjoining bathroom. "Something else" turned out to be Cade Landry. "What a jerk," she muttered as she yanked a brush through her slightly damp hair. Looking at her reflection, she added, "A gorgeous jerk, though."

She tossed her brush on the marble counter, then returned to her room and arranged three of the six pillows behind her. Her fingertip ran around the rim of her glass as her mind summoned his image. One minute he'd been giving her the full court press, next he'd accused her of murder, then he'd actually suggested she run off to the wilds of Montana with him.

"Definitely a jerk," she repeated as she took another swallow of wine. "A jerk who just saw his friend get murdered."

Barbara was annoyed with herself for feeling empathy for the man. Still, she knew how she'd felt more than a year earlier when she'd been locked in a room watching her friend die at the hands of a maniac. She'd been so crazy at the time that she'd actually risked physical danger in a failed attempt to save Claire.

"And I slapped the doctor who told me she was dead," Barbara recalled as a knot of emotion clogged her throat. "Not so different from Cade's reaction."

She finished her wine and got beneath the eyelet comforter. Maybe she was being too harsh on Landry. It didn't matter. She was fairly sure her hopes of getting the account had died with Dale. So much for going national, she thought as the music stopped and she closed her weary eyes.

IT'S JUST A DREAM. Barbara opened her eyes and squinted at the bright light from her bedside table lamp. She checked the clock and realized she'd been asleep for nearly two hours. Sleep and the residual fog of the two glasses of wine had her feeling a little fuzzy. Whatever sound she'd imagined in her dream couldn't have been real. She lay there quietly for more than a minute but heard nothing except the quiet whir of the ceiling fan.

She closed her eyes again. Relaxing against the pillows, she let out a small sigh. A second later, she bolted upright when the stereo blasted to life.

She scrambled out of bed and dashed for the stairs, wondering what she'd done to the state-of-the-art machine to make it come on again. Not only had it come on, it was playing a different CD. Harry Connick Jr.'s voice was loud enough to be deafening. She must have left it in the machine.

She was just steps away from the stereo when her mind registered the fact that the volume was on high. Even if she had somehow inadvertently set the timer, she knew she hadn't cranked up the volume.

Gripped by fear, she turned toward the door. A scream formed inside her chest when she saw the alarm keypad. The red light was off. A garbled sound escaped from her lips as she turned again. This time, she hurried toward the kitchen. She could hit the panic button by the back door and call for help.

Shoving aside the curtain, she pressed the red button, but it failed to start an alarm. Swallowing her panic, she reached for the phone at the same time as a gloved hand closed over her mouth.

She smelled and tasted leather as she was dragged against a hard form. She felt her feet dangling uselessly off the floor as she was yanked back toward the living room. In a matter of seconds, she was bashed against the wall, her masked attacker using his body to pin her in place. She struggled to free her arms and bit down hard on his gloved hand.

His expletive was muffled by the black ski mask

covering everything but his eyes. Eyes that were dark and lifeless. Barbara tried kicking and thrashing. As he eased off for a split second, she felt a glimmer of hope. Until she saw the glint of the knife blade before he pressed it to her throat.

His hand muted her cry. Wide-eyed, she was helpless to do anything as she felt the tip of the blade nick her skin. She was going to die.

The next thing she knew, the man had flown off her and she slumped to the floor clutching her throat. Involuntarily, she held her breath as she watched the attacker regain his footing and lunge at the other man. It took a full second for her to recognize her rescuer.

She managed to call out "Cade!" just as the attacker delivered a crushing punch to Cade's stomach. He doubled over yet somehow managed to swat the knife from the masked man. But in disarming the man, he had left his face unprotected. The attacker wasted no time. His fist came up, catching Cade in the chin with a blow that snapped Cade's head back and he staggered in her direction.

He teetered for a second, then landed on the floor with a loud thud just inches from her. As he tried to get his footing, the attacker delivered a swift kick to Cade's side before running out the front door.

Barbara scooted over to him, unsure how to help. "My God, Cade," she said on a rush of breath.

"Call the cops." Each word was uttered through pain-clenched teeth.

"Stay still," she said as she scrambled to the kitchen and lifted the receiver. The line was dead.

Glancing around the room, she saw a neat circle of glass had been cut from the back door, which was standing open. Ignoring the knowledge of how the man had made his entry, she grabbed her purse off the counter and dug out her cell phone. She called 911, then went back to tend to Cade.

She found him seated on the floor, his arms folded and resting on his knees. He was shaking his head as if to clear it.

"What are you doing here?" she asked as she grabbed the throw off the back of the sofa and used it to dab at the blood trickling from the corner of his mouth.

"I'd have thought you'd be right glad to see me, given the circumstances."

His nonchalant attitude was both soothing and annoying. "Of course I'm grateful," she said. "I just don't understand how you—" She went completely silent as he reached out and caught the lapels of her robe. Without a word, Cade pulled the edges together, then tightened the belt at her waist. Barbara felt her face flush as her eyes locked with his. "Sorry," she muttered.

He gave a guarded shake of his head and produced that sexy half smile. "Don't apologize. Knowing you don't have anything on under that robe was worth getting my ass kicked."

Barbara started to move back when he reached out

and caught the edge of her robe again. "Don't," she warned.

His smile broadened. "I just want to have a look at your neck."

She eyed him suspiciously. "Nice try, but..." She was rendered mute when his large, callused fingers gingerly touched her throat. When he pulled them away, she saw a small amount of blood on their blunt tips.

She was aware of so many things all at once. The uneven rhythm of his breathing. The sound of her own shallow breaths. The way his powerful thighs strained against the soft denim of his jeans. The small lines of concern at the corners of his mouth. Then, the wail of an approaching siren.

"It's nothing more than a scratch," he said as he started to stand.

"Don't get up until the paramedics get here," she insisted.

Not only did Cade ignore her, he rose and pulled her to her feet with almost no effort. "I'm fine."

"You were in a fight with a killer," Barbara argued. "You should stay still until we can get you to a hospital."

He grinned and winked. "I sure as hell don't need a hospital. I've gotten a worse licking than this just settling a disagreement with one of my cousins."

"Sounds like you have a lovely family."

"I do," he assured her. He hadn't dropped her

hand, and now Cade brought it up between them. "You're shaking."

"Duh?" she retorted incredulously as she made a futile attempt to regain her hand. The man was incredibly strong, yet he was looking at her with such tenderness. "Forgive me, but unlike you, when I see my cousins, we have tea."

"Cute," he said. "I'm sorry I didn't get here in time."

Tilting her head back, she looked into his eyes and realized his apology was genuine. "Why did you come here?"

"To watch you."

"I thought you were convinced I was responsible for Breck's murder."

He gave a small shrug. "I was. I came here tonight to see if I could catch you with Elvis."

Barbara ripped her hand from his grasp just as several police cars screeched to a halt outside her front door.

"Obviously, I've changed my mind," he said.

"Gee, thanks," she retorted as Dalton Ross came rushing inside.

"I knew this would happen," the detective seethed as he gripped her shoulder with one hand and tilted her chin with his thumb. After examining her wound, Dalton said, "It isn't deep."

Barbara patted his hand. "I'm not the one who got the brunt of it. Mr. Landry fought with the guy."

She followed Dalton's surprised eyes as he looked

at Cade, who was standing in the middle of her living room with his thumbs hooked in the belt loops of his jeans. "I guess I owe you one," Dalton said.

"No problem," Cade replied. "I'm just sorry the guy got away."

"Was it the same guy from the Rose Tattoo?" Dalton asked.

"It had to be," Barbara said.

Cade nodded in agreement as a paramedic went over to him and attempted to check his pulse. Cade shrugged him off. "I'm fine, pal."

"You should be examined," Barbara said.

Cade's eyes held hers. "Interested?"

"Not on your life," she retorted. "Who are all these people, Dalton?"

"Crime scene unit," he said as a small horde of uniformed men and women entered her condo.

"Waste of time," Cade commented. "The guy had on gloves and has to be a pro. He knew how to cut the phone line to override the alarm system and used a professional glass cutter to get in the back."

"That doesn't necessarily make him a pro," Dalton countered.

Cade shrugged. "Believe what you want. I still say he's some kind of professional killer."

"That may well be," Dalton admitted. "But we can't completely rule out other options. There have been some home invasions and sexual assaults in this general area."

Cade snorted. "Right. The fact that she witnessed a murder this evening can't be connected."

"I didn't say that," Dalton shot back defensively. "I was just pointing out that we have to consider all the possibilities."

"Then consider this," Cade retorted with equal ferocity. "If the guy wanted to rip her off, her purse was in the kitchen in plain sight. He could've cleaned out all the electronics on the first floor. Instead, he turned on the stereo to lure her downstairs. And," Cade continued, holding his hand up to silence Dalton, "if he just wanted to rape her, he probably wouldn't have tried to kill her first."

Barbara hugged herself. "I'm going to go upstairs and get dressed."

"I'll need your robe for forensics," Dalton said.

"Fine." Barbara raced from the room.

The detective turned to face Cade. "So what are you doing here?"

Cade didn't miss the subtle accusation in the man's voice. "I couldn't sleep."

"Try not to be a wiseass, Mr. Landry," Dalton warned. "I'm being nice because you apparently saved Barbara's life, but don't push me."

Cade squared off with the other man for a minute before saying, "Fair enough. I wanted to keep an eye on Miss Prather. Just in case she was involved in Dale's death."

Dalton seemed to consider his answer before giving

a slight nod of his head. "I told you there was no way she was involved."

"You were right. But I kinda like to find things out for myself."

Dalton gave instructions to one of the evidence technicians before turning his attention back to Cade. "So what can you tell me about the perp?"

Cade sat on the sofa and rubbed his face with his hands. "Medium height, but the guy's strong."

Barbara appeared on the stairs, looking anxious but stunning in a pair of black slacks and a charcoal-colored short-sleeved sweater with a high neckline. Cade guessed that she'd chosen the outfit to conceal the small cut on her throat. What he hadn't guessed was the intensity of his body's reaction to seeing her.

Her skin was pale and flawless. Her face was framed in a soft mass of unruly red hair. He wondered what it would be like to see that hair fanned out on his pillow. Her expression was an odd mixture of residual fear and quiet strength. Her body was simply incredible. He thought she was about five-six, but her small bone structure made her seem delicate. She was thin, but not so thin that she didn't have curves and contours that made a man think.

Of course, he didn't need much of an imagination. During her struggle with the hooded Elvis, her robe had opened and he'd gotten a guilty eyeful. If she only knew how much willpower it had taken for him to do the proper thing. Hell, he could still vividly remember the feel of the black silk and the warmth radiating from her perspiration-drenched skin. He figured those thoughts made him a first-class heel. He also felt sure the memory would be with him for a long time.

Barbara tossed a wad of black fabric at Dalton. "When forensics is finished with it, tell them to toss it."

Dalton nodded and handed the garment over to one of the evidence people. "Go ahead, Mr. Landry."

"Cade," he corrected automatically. "The guy was rock solid and sure as hell knew how to punch." Cade rubbed his chin. "I'm no stranger to fighting and neither was he."

Barbara took a seat in a floral-print chair across from him. He noted a slight tremor in her hands as she folded them neatly in her lap. The more gallant side of him wanted to pull her into his arms to make her feel safe. His intellect warned him that it probably wasn't such a good idea.

"How did you know Barbara was in trouble?" Dalton asked.

Cade kept his eyes on Barbara as he answered. "I was parked out front when I heard the stereo come on."

"He must have tried the bedroom door," Barbara mused. "When he found it was locked, he turned on the stereo so I'd come to him."

"All the lights were on in this side of the house, so I decided to go around back."

Dalton was taking notes while Cade spoke. "Did you see him in the house?" he asked.

"Not right off. The exterior electrical box was open and I saw the cut lines and the electrical override. When I got to the back door, I found it open and then I heard sounds of a struggle inside."

"Did you think to call the police?" Dalton asked.

Cade blew out a breath as he raked his hair back. "Gee, I can't say as I did. 'Course, that turned out to be a good thing since the guy was about to slit her throat when I showed up."

He watched as Barbara winced at his description.

"It wasn't a criticism, Cade," Dalton insisted. "I was just wondering why you would risk your own life for a stranger."

Cade laughed softly. "Where I come from, Detective, we watch out for our women."

"Is that before or after you drag them into your cave by the hair?" Barbara asked.

His laugh was more genuine this time. "Figure of speech. When you live in the shadow of the Rockies, you look out for your friends and neighbors. It's how we live."

Barbara looked appropriately chastised as she said, "I apologize for my curt remark. I really am glad you came along when you did, regardless of your reason for being outside my house."

Cade gave her his most practiced smile. "Good. Does that mean you're in my debt?"

She appeared startled by his question. "Of course. I suppose."

"I'll be sure to think of a way for you to repay me later," he said, enjoying the flash of anger in her blue eyes. He didn't stop to analyze why he liked goading this woman; he just knew he did. "I grabbed the guy. Got in maybe one solid one before he jabbed me in the gut, punched me in the face and kicked me in the ribs." Cade rubbed his tender side. "Not exactly my best showing, but I didn't expect a little guy to pack such power."

"Little?" Dalton asked.

"No more than five-ten or -eleven," Cade said.

"What about eye or hair color?"

"He was wearing a ski mask with the mouth opening sewn shut," Barbara said. "He had dark eyes. Really dark. Lifeless."

"Anything else?" Dalton prompted.

"Yeah," Cade answered. "His left eye is black."

"You got a good look at his eyes?" Dalton asked.

"Didn't need to," Cade responded. "I'm not talking about the color. I'm talking about the condition. I know I blackened the guy's eye. As they say, Elvis may have left the building, but he took one hell of a shiner with him."

Chapter Four

Barbara left the police department after the lunch hour and was surprised to find Cade Landry waiting for her. His face was partially obscured by the brim of a well-worn brown Stetson. All she could really see was his lopsided smile, but that was enough to make her heart skip a beat. Barbara told herself it was lack of sleep. She refused to even consider the possibility that she could be attracted to a man who used expressions like "our women."

"Couldn't find your way back to the airport?" she asked when she came to a halt a safe distance in front of him.

Tilting the hat back, he deepened his smile. "Now is that any way to greet the man who saved your sweet behind?"

"My, how you turn a phrase, Mr. Landry."

He didn't look the least bit repentant. In fact, he looked very pleased with himself. He smelled incredibly good. His cologne was subtle and masculine. "Subtle" wasn't an adjective she'd even consider when describing him, but "masculine" sure fit the bill. She guessed he was wearing the same jeans, but he'd changed into a fresh denim shirt that looked as soft and worn as his pants. The tips of his boots were scuffed and shaped by age and wear. He looked like...well, a cowboy.

"Ready to go?"

"Excuse me?" She blinked against the harsh sunlight as she spoke. "There has to be some mistake. Dalton said he arranged a ride for me."

"I rearranged your ride," he said without any apparent regard for her plans or desires.

"I think you've already done enough on my behalf."

"Not by my way of thinking," he said as he opened the door of a navy sedan. "Get on in."

Barbara hesitated. "I'm not sure this is such a good idea."

"I don't bite," he said. When she slipped into the passenger seat, he bent forward and added, "hard."

"Look," Barbara began when he slid behind the wheel, "I've been generous in overlooking your come-ons out of deference for your loss." She watched as her statement erased the amusement from his chiseled features. "But you have to stop. I'm really not comfortable with the way you talk to me."

"Why?"

"Why?" she parroted. "Because you're a potential

client, so our conversations should remain professional.''

"Professional, huh?" Cade stroked the shadow of a beard on his chin. "Was it professional for me to risk great bodily injury to keep you from getting your throat cut last night?"

Barbara closed her eyes and summoned patience. "I've already told you how much I appreciate—"

"I don't want your appreciation," he said.

Barbara stiffened. "If you think I'll invite you back to my place for a quick tumble, you're sadly mistaken."

His laughter mocked all her grand hauteur. Cade turned in the seat and caught her chin between his thumb and forefinger. Gently but with determination, he forced her to face him. She was surprised at the fierceness that had turned his eyes as dark gray as a threatening thundercloud. His mouth was little more than a thin, angry line. Barbara opened her mouth, but a slight movement of his head warned her against speaking just yet.

"First, I don't need you to keep thanking me. I was just glad I was there before things got really ugly."

"I do app—"

"Second," he cut in with a voice deepened by controlled anger, "contrary to what you think, I'm capable of separating our professional relationship from anything else. Prather and Associates has business with the cartel. You'll get a fair shake from me."

Barbara jerked her face free but glared up at him. "Anything else?"

He reached up and allowed the pad of his forefinger to trace a slow path along her jawline. "Yeah." His voice was softer, almost hypnotic, when the anger drained from his eyes. "You and I are people, not businesses. When we end up in bed together, it won't have anything to do with ad campaigns, and it sure as hell won't be quick."

"When?" she challenged, unable to let the comment pass.

He rolled his eyes. "I'm not real big on games, Barbara."

It shouldn't have mattered that he had just used her name for the first time. It should only matter that the man had made a blatant sexual reference that was completely unacceptable. *Really? Then why is your stomach quivering?* "I'm not playing any game."

"Right," he sighed as he turned the key in the ignition. "If it makes you feel better to tell yourself you aren't interested in me, feel free."

"I'm grateful to you," Barbara insisted. "After what happened with Claire, I empathize with how you feel about Mr. Breck's murder. I know—"

"Do you really want me to get mad?" he asked, one brow arched toward the brim of his hat.

"I want you to understand that we are not going to explore any relationship outside of—"

"Speak for yourself," he said as he put the car in gear and drove out of the parking lot. "I figure it's my prerogative as a man to see if I can light your fire.''

''A *cave*man, maybe.'' Barbara sat back in her seat as they drove through the narrow streets of downtown Charleston.

''How do you stand all this damned traffic?'' he grumbled when he found himself forced to merge to the left by the medical center.

''I don't get lost,'' Barbara said, enjoying the fact that he'd missed the exit that would have taken him up to I-526.

''I'm not lost.''

''Yes, you are. My condo is back the other way. We can go up to 17 and turn around.''

''We're going the right way.''

''Trust me, Landry. My condo is north of the city.''

''I know, but my plane is at the Executive Airport near Folly Beach.''

''And you think I have nothing better to do than return your rental car?'' she asked, very affronted.

''Nope. You're coming with me.''

''You're mentally unbalanced.''

Cade gave her that killer half smile. ''No, darlin'. Elvis is mentally unbalanced. You, on the other hand, are a target. Dalton and I agreed that this was for the best.''

''Dalton wouldn't do this to me.''

''Think not? Feel free to give him a call.''

Barbara pulled her cell phone from her purse and

did exactly that. Dalton answered on the first ring. "What's going on?" she demanded.

"I guess this means Landry picked you up."

She glanced over to see him grinning from ear to ear. "You're supposed to be my friend, Dalton. Why didn't you discuss this with me when I was in your office?"

"Because I knew you wouldn't go along with me. I also know how, er, persuasive Landry can be."

"This is not acceptable, Dalton. I can't run off to the wilds of Montana. I have a business. Responsibilities."

"So do I, Barbara. First and foremost, I have a responsibility to keep you alive. Getting you out of town is the safest option. Elvis knew where you lived less than two hours after he hit Breck. I'm sure by now he knows where you work, where you shop and when you eat dinner. If you don't want to go with Landry, I'll have one of my officers take you to a safe house. What I won't do is allow your sense of independence to get you killed. Which will it be?"

She let out a frustrated groan. "Is there something in column C?"

Dalton laughed. "Please, Barbara. Give me a break and cooperate. If anything happens to you, Haley will be devastated. Just go to Montana and wow the cowboys with your ideas. Consider it a business trip."

"This is crazy," she complained. Then, looking purposefully at Cade, she added, "How do you know

Landry isn't some sort of serial killer?'' Her question caused him to raise an eyebrow.

"I checked him out,'' Dalton said. "He doesn't so much as have a traffic ticket. Hell, his cousin is the sheriff of Jasper.''

"Jasper?'' she repeated.

"His ranch is outside of a town named Jasper.''

"How quaint,'' she said with saccharine sweetness. "I'll go on one condition.''

"Name it.''

"I'm putting Landry on the phone and I want you to make sure he understands this is a business trip.'' Barbara shoved the phone at him. She held it to his ear while he muttered a series of affirmative grunts and groans. She put the phone back to her ear and said, "Do we understand each other?''

"He's a nice guy,'' Dalton assured her. "Give him a break and try to enjoy yourself.''

"Right.''

"Haley says she'll call you.''

"How does Haley know I'm going to Montana?'' Barbara asked.

"I might have mentioned it after I made arrangements with Landry this morning.''

"This morning?'' Barbara repeated, then replayed the day in her mind. "Are you telling me that I spent hours pouring over mug shots just so you and Landry could plan all this?''

"Pretty much,'' Dalton admitted. "I also needed

some time to check him out and he needed time to swing by your place and get your stuff."

"My stuff?"

"He went by the condo to pack your bag."

"Remind me to kill you when I get back, Dalton." Angrily, she snapped the phone closed and threw it into her bag. "You packed for me?"

He nodded as he pulled into the private airstrip and parked next to a hangar with a neatly painted sign indicating the flight office.

"Don't worry," he said as he stepped from the car and went to the trunk.

Barbara scrambled out and followed him. "Forgive me, but I can't believe you'd have the first clue what to pack. You'll have to take me back to my house and then to my office."

"Sorry," he said as he lifted two suitcases she recognized as her own out of the trunk. He then grabbed a flight bag and started toward the office.

"What do you mean 'sorry'?" she demanded as she struggled to keep up with his long, purposeful strides. "There are certain things I need, and I can't very well show you my ideas if I don't have the presentation from my office."

"You can have your secretary send it to you at the ranch," he said before he stuck his head inside the office door and yelled, "I left the keys in the car. Thanks."

"No problem, Mr. Landry. I filed your flight plans straight through. The latest Doppler and NWS reports are already in your cockpit!'' came the faceless reply. ''Y'all have a safe trip home.''

He gave her no choice but to follow him to continue her appeal. ''Wait, for goodness' sake! Where are the others?''

''They took a commercial flight earlier,'' Cade explained. ''But don't worry, you'll have time to present your ideas to the full cartel board.''

''At least take me back to my place so I can get some clothes and—''

''I packed your clothes,'' he said as he walked to an impressive private jet waiting on the runway.

''Forgive me, but you're a rancher, not a fashion consultant. I hardly think you're qualified—'' she paused long enough to climb inside the plane with him ''—to select my wardrobe.''

''You'd be surprised,'' he said. After latching the door, he stowed the luggage in compartments above the six seats in the passenger section. ''Until recently, I've been packing Jessica's clothes.''

''Jessica?''

''My daughter.''

''That's all well and good, but I don't wear color coordinated play sets.''

Apparently ignoring her, he sat down and fastened his seat belt, then started flipping switches and pushing buttons. ''You need to buckle up.''

''But—''

''It's the law.''

Barbara fell into the seat next to his and buckled

her seat belt. "Has anyone ever told you how incredibly pushy you are?"

"Not this week," he admitted as the plane's engines whirred to life. "Jessica has been busy."

"Finger painting?" Barbara suggested. "You really can't compare me to your daughter, Landry. Which gets us back to the issue of my clothing needs."

"You don't have any needs," he said with a laugh. "You have more clothes in your closet than all the shops in Jasper put together."

"You had no business going into my home without my permission."

The plane rolled down the runway, then lifted weightlessly into the clear blue sky. She clutched the side of her seat as he banked the small plane.

"Don't tell me you're afraid to fly."

Barbara loosened her grip. "I'm not afraid to fly. I just have never been in the driver's seat before."

"Copilot's seat," he corrected easily. "Don't worry, I won't need your help on anything but the landing."

She glared at him, knowing full well he didn't need her help. "I have to tell you, I really resent you and Dalton plotting against me like this."

He flipped a few more switches and stretched his legs. "Would you rather stay in Charleston and wait for Elvis to pay you another visit?"

"Of course not. But I'm also not fond of the idea of being in the middle of nowhere with a sexist rancher. I could've taken a vacation, gone somewhere."

His expression grew serious. "Dalton and I agreed that Elvis is enough of a pro to trace you. Probably through your credit cards. This way, no one knows where you are and it's less likely Elvis will connect the two of us. Even if he does, my ranch is completely safe."

"What about your daughter?" Barbara asked. "Aren't you putting her safety at risk by bringing me to your ranch?"

"Jess lives in Helena during the week."

"Great parenting," Barbara commented acerbically.

Cade cast her a withering stare. "Don't cross that line, lady. My daughter goes to school in Helena and lives with her maternal grandparents."

"Is her mother too busy to take care of her?"

"Her mother is dead."

"I'm sorry," Barbara said in earnest. "I didn't realize you were a widower."

"I'm not. My wife and I divorced a few years before she died in a car accident. My in-laws took it hard. Having Jess with them during the week helps them and it allows Jess to attend a decent school in the city. Everybody's happy."

Somehow Barbara wasn't convinced. "Isn't it hard on a little girl to be shuffled back and forth like that?"

He laughed. "Jess is sixteen."

"Started young, huh?"

"Twenty-five. You'll like Jess. The two of you are both spoiled brats."

"I'm not spoiled and I can't picture you spoiling your child."

"I don't. Her grandparents do." Cade reached behind him and opened a small refrigerator, then pulled out two bottles of water. "They've recently decided that Jess should stay in the city on the weekends to meet decent boys."

"Your scowl tells me you don't approve."

"She already thinks she's sixteen going on forty-five. She needs to study, not worry about boys and cars."

"Don't worry, Landry. It isn't dangerous until she's concerned about being *in* a car *with* a boy. So long as she keeps the two separate, you're home free."

"That's comforting," he groaned. "Do me a favor and don't encourage her."

"Suppose I'll corrupt her thinking?"

Cade turned and met her gaze. "Any woman with as much sexy lingerie as you have can't be a good influence."

She felt her face flush. "A true gentleman wouldn't have commented on my unmentionables."

"Then I'm very glad I'm not a true gentleman."

Chapter Five

"Welcome to the Lazy L," Cade said as he taxied the plane to a stop.

Barbara looked around. Wisps of soft white clouds embellished the brilliant blue sky. When the door to the plane was open, she breathed in fresh, clean air. "This is very different from Charleston," she commented.

"No pollution, no noise," Cade added.

"No ranch," Barbara responded dryly.

He glanced over his shoulder as he preceded her out of the plane. "Watch your step," he cautioned.

"Welcome home, Boss."

Barbara stepped out from behind Cade and was greeted by a pair of wary but curious brown eyes. She guessed the man was over sixty. Either that, or life in Montana caused premature aging. He offered a hand gnarled by age or arthritis.

"Slick Drummond, ma'am."

"Barbara Prather," she returned as she accepted his firm handshake.

Slick pushed his hat back on his forehead and looked at Cade. Some sort of silent communication passed between the two of them before Slick took one of the suitcases and shuffled over to one of two waiting four-wheel drives.

After he and Cade loaded the suitcases in the first vehicle, Slick got behind the wheel while Cade held open the door of the second car for her.

"I hate to sound obtuse," Barbara said, "but where is the ranch?"

Cade laughed. "We're on it."

She peered ahead and saw nothing but fenced prairie until the tall grasses met the Rocky Mountains. "Doesn't a ranch normally have some cows and a ranch house?" she queried.

Cade started the Bronco's engine. "The house is about five miles to the west."

Barbara sat up straighter. "Wouldn't it make more sense to put your airstrip close to your house?"

He shrugged. The action caused his shirt to pull taut across the vast expanse of his chest. Barbara was uncomfortably aware of the fact that Cade's inherent masculinity seemed to push all her buttons. As if her ability to control her own brain had suddenly evaporated, she couldn't stop noticing things about this man. His skin was deeply tanned, hugely in contrast to her very pale, typically redhead complexion. Even in profile, there was a quiet strength in his face. He wasn't classically handsome, but he was definitely ruggedly gorgeous. She guessed he'd broken his nose a time or two. There was also a faded scar on his right hand just below his knuckles.

"'Sides, the helicopters make too much noise," he explained.

Barbara considered his answer. "You have a private jet *and* helicopters?"

"Yep."

She twisted a lock of hair around her finger. "I take it you like to fly."

"I do, but the helicopters aren't for pleasure flying. We use them to locate and move cattle."

"I thought all a cowboy needed was a well-trained horse, a dog and some rope."

"Twenty years ago, maybe," he agreed. "Now we rely on technology just like the rest of the world."

Barbara remained quiet for a few minutes. She divided her attention between the incredible landscape and Cade as he smoothly steered the car along the unpaved and somewhat rutted road. In the distance, a series of buildings began to pop into view. Cade's whole demeanor seemed to change as the house and other buildings appeared. The small lines at the corners of his mouth and eyes relaxed.

"What's that?" she asked as they passed a series of fenced pens.

"Corrals. Over there—" he pointed to a building that reminded her of the lean-tos she'd built at camp as a child "—are the calving barns."

"Again," Barbara began cautiously, "not to sound stupid, but where are the cows?"

His chuckle was deep. "North pastures," he explained. "We can ride out tomorrow if you'd like to see them."

"Ride what?" she asked. "Helicopters?"

He tossed her an amused glance. "Horses."

Barbara almost shuddered at the thought. "I don't ride."

"Then I'll teach you."

"Pass, thanks. My father was under the mistaken impression that I should learn dressage as a child."

"And you fell off a horse and never got back on?"

She shook her head. "I never got on in the first place. I spent six weeks in the high country of South Carolina at an incredibly expensive stable and never once got in the saddle."

"Why not?" he asked as they passed through a beautiful white archway onto a semicircular-shaped driveway in front of a rustic but impressive home.

"I have a serious horse phobia."

"We can fix that," he assured her.

"No thanks." Cade brought the car to a stop behind a small red sports car. "I wouldn't have pegged you as the Miata type," she said.

"I'm not," he replied. His expression grew hard.

Barbara was suddenly gripped by fear. "You don't think Elvis has found—"

He placed his hand on her thigh. "Don't panic. It doesn't belong to a killer, but I will kill the person who bought it."

No sooner had the words left his mouth than the

front door opened and a tall, thin girl bounded from the house. Barbara was certain the girl had to be Cade's daughter. She had his distinctive gray-green eyes.

"Daddy!" the girl cried as she gave the big man a hug even before he was fully out of the car. The girl's enthusiasm waned when she spotted Barbara. "Who's she?"

Nice to meet you, too, Barbara thought.

"This is Barbara Prather. She's an ad executive from Charleston. Barbara, this is Jessica."

"Is she staying long?" Jessica asked as she gave Barbara a very unwelcoming glare. "I came home to be with you because of Uncle Dale and all."

Ignoring his daughter's bad manners, Cade left one arm draped over the girl as he steered her toward the sports car. "What's this?"

Jessica managed to beam and look innocent all at one time. "We talked about this, Daddy. Granddad and Grans thought I needed a car and—"

"I said no," Cade finished. "You aren't keeping this."

Jessica pursed her lips. "Grans said you were being unreasonable. All the girls my age at school have cars."

"I'm sure," Cade said. "But I don't think you're ready for the responsibility of a car yet."

"Get real, Daddy," she said as she snaked one arm through his. "It's just a car. It isn't like I brought some strange guy home and had sex." The latter part of her remark was punctuated with an accusatory look in Barbara's direction.

"Watch yourself," Cade warned. "Barbara is here to work."

"I'm sure," Jessica purred. "So am I. Grans said I could miss this week at school to help you with the funeral and all."

Barbara watched as Cade rubbed his hands over his face. "You are not going to miss an entire week of school. In fact, I want you to go back to Helena tonight."

Jessica planted her feet one step above her father. "I don't want to go back tonight!" she wailed. "I need to be with you, Daddy."

Cade hugged his child. "I know how much you loved Dale."

"I did," Jessica agreed with a little sob. "I can't believe he's dead."

I can't believe you're falling for this, Barbara thought, recognizing the manipulative tactic she'd used on her own father. Most young girls learned early on that the way to a father's heart was tears. Fathers couldn't handle tears.

"Still," Cade said as he kissed Jess's forehead, "I want you back in Helena."

Good for you, Barbara thought. *Stand firm or she'll run right over you.*

"But—"

"No argument," Cade insisted. "We'll have dinner together, then I'll have Slick follow you back to your grandparents' house.''

Apparently, Jessica knew when not to press her father. She didn't seem to have the same knowledge when it came to Barbara.

''Will *she* be eating with us?'' Jessica asked, making the word ''she'' sound like a vile curse.

''Feel free to call me Barbara.''

''Will she?'' Jess asked again.

''Yes,'' Cade answered. ''Remember your manners.''

''I'm sorry, Daddy,'' Jess purred. ''I guess I'm just *soooo* upset about Uncle Dale. I just don't know what I'm saying.''

Right, Barbara silently fumed. This kid was some piece of work. She was rude, pouty, selfish and manipulative. Barbara recognized those traits because she had possessed them herself at one time. She'd spent much of her young life sabotaging her father's relationships. She regretted it now.

A woman stood at the open doorway. Smiling, she said, ''Welcome home, Cade.'' The smile faded as she turned to Barbara. ''You must be Miss Prather?''

Barbara was taken aback by the frosty greeting. Between the two females, she felt as welcome as invading bacteria. Forcing a smile to her lips, she said, ''Hello.''

''This is Mrs. Granger,'' Cade said. ''She's the only thing standing between me and TV dinners.''

The woman scoffed. ''I'm the only thing standing

between him and filth. If I didn't pick up after this boy, we'd be knee-deep in dirty socks.''

"Is that so?" Barbara asked, amused.

"It *was* so," Cade replied with mock defensiveness. "I was a bit of a slob in my teens and she's never forgiven me."

Mrs. Granger's faded blue eyes filed with sadness. "I've taken care of the things you requested on the phone."

"Thanks," Cade said. Pain flashed across his handsome face. "I'd like an early dinner. Barbara's on east-coast time and I want Jess to have plenty of time to drive that fancy car of hers back to Helena before it gets too late."

"Then I can keep it?" Jess squealed triumphantly.

Cade shrugged. "The jury's still out."

"I'll be really responsible, Daddy. Besides, with my own car, I can come and visit you more often."

Cade shook his head. "You will not. In fact, I want you to stay in Helena the next few weekends."

At first the girl looked heartbroken, then she turned venomous eyes on Barbara. "Are you going to be too busy for your own daughter?"

Cade gave the girl a gentle, one-armed hug. "I've got a lot of business to take care of here and for the cartel. Besides, your grandmother said she thought you should spend more time socializing with your schoolmates."

Jess's eyes glistened with anger. "Grans wants me to go out with Steven Bixby."

"Is that the end of the world?" Cade asked.

Jess let out an exasperated breath. "Big time! Steven Bixby is just a boy. Grans only wants me to go out with him because his family has money and she says he's a good catch."

"You're only sixteen," Cade said. "You've got years before you start worrying about catching anyone."

"Grans said Momma fell in love with you when she was my age."

"Your grandmother talks too much," Cade commented as he gave the girl a gentle swat. "Go on and get your things together. I'll make arrangements for you to come to Dale's funeral later on this week."

Jessica marched haughtily toward a polished oak staircase to the left of the entry foyer.

Shaking his head, Cade turned to Barbara. "Sorry."

Barbara shrugged and offered him an understanding smile. "No problem," she assured him. "I was sixteen once."

He nodded. "Mrs. Granger, please take Barbara to the blue guest room." Barbara caught Mrs. Granger's moment of surprise before she averted her eyes. Cade sighed and said, "I'll see you at dinner."

Barbara followed the housekeeper up the gleaming staircase to a second-floor hallway. The house appeared to be a generous H shape. The older woman led her to the second door on the left of the main hall. After ushering Barbara inside, she went to the window and raised the shade, filling the room with rays of prismed sunlight. It was a spacious and homey room with dark, rustic wood furniture softened by feminine touches of robin's-egg blue.

Mrs. Granger asked to be excused for a moment, leaving Barbara to explore the room. A large iron bed dominated one wall. She stepped forward and ran her fingers over the hand-stitched quilt covering the bed. Someone had taken the time to fashion matching shams for the pillows, and judging by the slight fading of the quilt, Barbara guessed it was an heirloom.

She felt tired and sluggish, probably a result of the events of the past twenty-four hours as well as the time difference. Given her druthers, she would have gladly curled up on the bed to treat her sleep deprivation. The room had what she assumed were two closets. There was a door on either side of the headboard. The decor included an oak dresser and washstand, complete with a flow-blue bowl and pitcher. She smiled, thinking how very different this place was from her high-tech condo. Then she frowned, wondering why she found the quaint surroundings so appealing. *Has to be a brain freeze from lack of sleep.*

When Mrs. Granger returned, she was carrying both of Barbara's suitcases.

"Let me help you," Barbara insisted, rising to take the larger one. Sensing disapproval from the woman, Barbara busied herself by setting the suitcase on the floor next to an antique Arts and Crafts oval mirror. Hoping the best way to resolve this conflict was the direct approach, she caught the other woman's eye and asked, "Have I offended you?"

"No, Miss Prather."

Formal, stiff, guarded answer, she thought. "Coming here wasn't my idea."

Mrs. Granger lifted one gray eyebrow questioningly. "Cade can be...persuasive."

"Cade can be overbearing," Barbara countered wryly. "I only came so that I could get the cartel account."

The housekeeper appeared to consider her comment. "I see."

Somehow "I see" sounded a lot like "Yeah, right," and that rankled. "Mrs. Granger," Barbara began in a tone she hadn't used since addressing her father's staff years ago, "I'm sorry my presence seems to have upset you and Cade's daughter. But I can assure you, I'm only interested in landing the account."

Mrs. Granger shrugged. "I understand."

Barbara sighed in frustration. "Then why do I get the distinct feeling that I'm intruding on holy ground?"

The woman dipped her head in a subservient fashion. "That wasn't my intention, miss. Would you like for me to unpack for you now, or would you prefer to rest first?"

"I'll unpack, thank you," Barbara answered in surrender. She was too exhausted to split hairs.

Mrs. Granger went to the door to the right of the

bed and pulled it open. "There are hangers in here
and the dresser is empty. If you need—"

"I know how to unpack," Barbara assured her.
"Thank you."

Once the housekeeper left, Barbara opened her suitcases and surveyed the contents. Her clothing was
neatly arranged and surprisingly complete, and her
toiletry bag contained makeup and bathroom essentials. As far as she could tell, the only area where
Cade had dropped the ball was accessories. There
wasn't a necklace or a pair of earrings to be found.
Not that it really mattered. Cade had packed her casual things, no suits. The ranch was obviously an in-
formal place and she didn't intend on staying very
long. "Not after getting such a cool reception from
Jess and Mrs. Granger," she muttered as she set to
work.

BARBARA WAS JOLTED AWAKE ninety minutes later by
a flying pillow. After brushing it aside, she looked
into the cool eyes of Jess.

"Dinner in ten minutes," the surly teenager announced.

"Thanks," Barbara responded. "Do you always
throw things at virtual strangers?"

"Only the ones sleeping with my dad."

Barbara sat up, rubbing her face in the process. "I
hate to disappoint you, Jess, but I'm not sleeping with
your father. I'm here on business."

"Sure you are," she sneered as she dramatically

placed one hand on a slim hip. "I guess that's why my dad is making me go back to Helena with Slick as my escort tonight. And my name is Jessica. Only my friends call me Jess."

Barbara silently reminded herself that she had been just like the girl once upon a time. "Well then, *Jessica,* I repeat, I am here on business, period."

The girl rolled her eyes. "I'm not a baby. I know what sexual chemistry is."

Barbara got out of bed and was sorry that she fell short of being eye level with the girl. It would have been more effective had she been able to look down from a position of authority. "Sexual chemistry?"

"Sure," Jessica lashed out as she jammed her hands into the pockets of her jeans. "I've seen my father with women before. And I recognize sexual chemistry."

"Even if there was some sort of chemistry between your father and me—which there isn't," Barbara insisted, "I won't be going to the lab to test it. I'm here on business."

"You're a liar. Dad wouldn't have asked Mrs. Granger to put you in *this* room if you were only here on business." Jessica gave her a withering glare before adding, "There's a bathroom across the hall."

Once the girl had stomped off, Barbara went to the bathroom to splash some water on her hot face. "That girl is a spoiled little snot," she muttered as she dug into her makeup bag and found a brush. Her conscience added, *Takes one to know one.*

By the time she'd retouched her makeup and gone downstairs, nearly twenty minutes had passed. A fact that hadn't been lost on the housekeeper, who refused to even look in her direction.

Cade was doing the exact opposite. His gray-green eyes boldly roamed the full length of her body as he rose to offer her the seat to his left. Barbara felt like kicking him. His once-over hadn't gone unnoticed by his daughter, which was sure to add fuel to her mistaken suspicions.

Barbara accepted the seat and told herself she didn't even notice the smell of his soap or the snug fit of his jeans as he returned to his chair. His perfectly shaped derriere wasn't any of her concern. Nor did she care that the top three buttons of his shirt had been left undone, revealing soft, dark hair covering the hard outline of his well-muscled chest.

"Hungry?"

Barbara felt her eyes grow wide with guilt.

"Hello? How lame, Daddy. Look at the way she's staring at you," Jessica muttered.

"Jess," Cade said as warning. "That's enough."

The girl simply shrugged, then grabbed a bowl of broccoli and heaped a large amount in the center of her plate. "I'm sorry, Daddy."

"I'm not the one you should be saying that to."

Barbara watched the silent clash of wills as Cade and his daughter engaged each other silently. The air in the large room felt tense and close. It was a sadly familiar feeling, one she had no intention of perpetuating.

"No apology necessary," she said, passing a plate of steaks to Jessica. When the girl refused to accept the platter, Barbara simply placed it in the center of the table. "I used to think the same things when my father had female guests to the house."

"We aren't going to bond, so you can skip any speeches on ways we're alike, Miss Prather," Jessica countered.

Seeing anger rise in Cade's eyes, Barbara reached beneath the table and touched his knee before saying, "You're quite right, Jessica. I won't be around long enough for us to bond."

"You think that makes you unique?" Jessica asked. "Daddy never keeps women around very long."

"That is quite enough," Cade exploded. "You will apologize and then you will keep your mouth shut until it's time for you to leave."

Jessica just shrugged and began to eat.

It was amazing that Barbara was able to swallow with the lump of uneasiness in her throat. The situation was only made worse by the fact that neither Cade nor his daughter spoke during the meal. The only sounds in the house emanated from the kitchen, which was precisely where Barbara headed as soon as possible.

"Mrs. Granger will get the dishes," Cade said.

Meeting his eye, she said, "I'll give her a hand so

that you and your daughter can spend some time together before she leaves.''

"Nice touch," Jessica mumbled.

Barbara smiled at her. "Thanks, I thought so."

Balancing her plate and the meat platter in one hand, she went through the hinged door into the kitchen. Two things happened almost immediately. Mrs. Granger scrambled from her place at the kitchen table and Cade's voice thundered to life.

"I'll take those, miss."

Barbara shook her head. "No."

The housekeeper slowly returned to her seat.

"Why can't T.J. follow me?" Jessica screamed in the adjoining room.

"Getting out of the battle zone?" the housekeeper asked.

"I'm not stupid, Jess," Cade yelled back. "I've seen the way you throw yourself at him. You seem to forget that you're only sixteen and T.J. works for me. He's a ranch hand, for God's sake!"

Barbara went to the sink and turned on the faucet in hopes of drowning out the argument. It was futile. Cade had obviously passed his stubborn temper on to his only child.

"You were working on Uncle Caleb's ranch when you and Momma fell in love!" Jessica fired back.

"That was different."

"Right, Daddy. You won't even let me go to the movies with T.J. It isn't fair."

"Life isn't fair, Jess," Cade said in a somewhat

softer tone. "I don't want to see you make the same mistakes I did."

"So now you're saying I was a mistake?"

"I did not say that. You know you're the most important thing in my life."

"I guess that's why *she* gets to stay here and I have to go back to that nasty school."

"You have to go back to school because that's your job," Cade said. "One more crack about Miss Prather and that spiffy car your grandparents bought will be history."

"Daaady!"

"I mean it, Jess. I want you to put a smile on your pretty face and your things in the car."

Barbara heard a chair scrape the wood floor in the dining room and figured round one was over. She just wasn't sure who had won.

Chapter Six

Cade paced the full length of the porch sipping beer from a long-necked bottle. He was tired and wired all at the same time and hoped the alcohol would put him back on an even keel. Fighting with Jess hadn't done him any good. Worse still, he hated himself for lying to her. He'd always prided himself on being honest with his daughter, and for the foreseeable future, he would have to rely on deception if his plan was going to work.

Jess wasn't the only one he was lying to. He took a long pull on the bottle and let the bitter drink burn his throat. His life was suddenly very complicated.

"Drinking alone?"

He turned and found Barbara standing just outside the doorway. Though he knew better, Cade indulged himself by letting his eyes get their fill. The reprimand in her expression couldn't deter him. It was just too damn nice looking at the way her sweater hugged her curves. The woman had a body that wouldn't quit. Just being in close proximity to her seemed to make his breath catch in his chest. Maybe he'd been too long without a woman. He considered that possibility as he took in her wild red hair and sparkling blue eyes. No. This wasn't about *a* woman. It was about *this* woman.

"Want one?" he asked in cautioned syllables.

She arched one perfectly shaped brow. "One what?"

He had to smile at her directness. Cocking his head to one side, he said, "Lady's choice."

He watched as her shoulders seemed to relax.

"A drink would probably put me in a coma," she answered. "I'm battling the urge to crawl into bed as it is."

"You don't have to keep me company," he said just as a breeze kicked up and treated him to a whiff of her perfume.

"I wasn't planning on it. I'm trying to stay awake so that I can adjust to the time difference."

"There's plenty of time for that."

She shook her head. "I'm not staying long. I don't function very well in battle zones."

Cade had to smile before finishing off his beer. After tossing the bottle into a nearby recycling bin, he turned and braced his hands on the split-wood railing. "I'm sorry my daughter was such a pain."

She came to stand near him. It bothered him that Barbara wasn't closer. The foot or so between them seemed like miles. "Let's not forget your housekeeper. Mrs. Granger didn't exactly take to me, either.''

"She's cautious."

"Whatever," Barbara said.

He noticed that her voice was deep and throaty. The kind of voice a man fantasized about on long, cold nights. Her profile was almost as pretty as her face, he decided when he leaned back. The moonlight did something wonderful to her skin. It gave her the look of a fine porcelain sculpture. A sculpture he wanted to run his hands over.

"I have a proposition for you."

His body stirred. "Shoot."

"If I can find out why Dale was killed, will you give me a fair chance at the cartel account?"

He gaped at her. "You're talking a business proposition?"

She offered him a charming smile. "Of course. If I'm successful, we both get what we want."

"I'm going to give you a fair shake," he said. "I already told you that. Now, as for delving into why Dale was killed, forget it."

"Why?" she demanded, fire in her eyes. Raising one hand before he could speak, she added, "Besides, I couldn't forget it even if I tried. The man was shot right in front of *me* and Elvis showed up in *my* bedroom with a knife."

"Which is exactly why you will hang back and let the authorities handle this. You aren't going to look into anything while you're under my roof."

Her body took on a rigid, challenging stance. "I didn't ask to be under your roof! I'd gladly go back to civilization this instant."

Anger flashed hotly inside his gut. "What about Elvis?"

"He can't be stupid enough to come after me again. I'm not afraid of him."

With speed and agility, Cade lifted her against him hard. He felt the breath rush from her body as he looked down at her shocked expression. "I fought with Elvis, remember?" he reminded her. "The guy was as strong as a bull."

"Big deal," she spit out as she struggled in his hold. "Let me go this second!"

"Is that how you plan on handling Elvis?"

She glared up at him and went completely still in his arms. "I plan on being smarter than Elvis. Brains over brawn. Ever heard that expression?"

He brought his face closer to hers. "Beaten into submission. Ever hear that one?"

"You're pushing me, Landry. Stop acting like some prehistoric cretin."

"Cretin?" he repeated with a laugh. "I was making a point."

She stared at him through thick lashes. "So am I. I don't like your tactics. I sure as hell don't like being manhandled."

"Maybe it's time you gave it a try." He shifted his hold on her slightly. He was no longer gripping her like an attacker. He was holding her the way a man was meant to hold a woman. He felt her softness and her heat. It hit him like a fist in the gut. As he gazed down at her slightly parted lips, his fingers laced up through her hair. Applying just a fraction of pressure, he was able to place her mouth just beneath his own. Desire and need welled inside him. He wanted her as much as he wanted his next breath. It was so overwhelming that he almost missed the look in her eyes. Seeing it, he released her in an instant.

Turning, he raked his hands through his hair and let out a muffled curse. "Go in the house, Barbara."

"No."

He felt like punching something. "I'm not up for trading barbs with you right now, so please leave."

"No."

He glowered at her, annoyed that she looked so calm while he felt so out of control. "I apologize. I was out of line. Now will you go in the house?"

She pushed her hair away from her face as she held her ground. "An apology isn't enough."

"Well, it's the best I have to offer."

She shook her head. "Not in my experience."

Ramming the heels of his hands against his eyes, he willed himself back into control. "What do you want?"

She stepped closer. "I want your word that nothing like this will ever happen again."

"Fine."

"I mean it, Landry. I have no desire to be treated like some cheap entertainment. Coming here wasn't my idea. I want the account, but I won't have sex with you to get it.''

"I wouldn't ask you to.''

"You weren't *asking* a minute ago. You were taking.''

"It won't happen again,'' he said as he stepped off the porch and strode toward the paddock.

"GOOD MORNING.''

"It's almost noon,'' her secretary, Tracey, said. "You won't believe what happened and where the hell are you? I've been calling you for hours.''

"I'm in Montana,'' she said. "What's the matter? You sound upset.''

"I am upset!'' Tracey wailed. "Everything is destroyed.''

"What everything?'' Barbara asked, knowing full well her secretary was given to great melodrama.

"The office. He trashed everything.''

"What?'' she yelled just as Cade entered the kitchen and went to the coffeepot. "What happened?''

"I'll put Dalton on the line. He can tell you.''

Cade gave her a questioning look while she waited for Dalton to explain. He looked tired and that gave her a small measure of satisfaction. She hoped he felt like a total creep after the way he'd treated her on the porch.

She certainly felt like a creep. Instead of wanting to slap him, she could only focus on the fact that his shirt wasn't buttoned and his hair was still wet from the shower. Small droplets of water trickled down through the mat of rich, dark hair covering his chest. The hair tapered into a tight vee before disappearing into the waistband of his jeans. When he reached for a mug from the cabinet, her eyes feasted on rippling stomach muscles.

"How are you doing?" Dalton asked.

"I've lost my mind," Barbara answered with a fair amount of self-loathing. "What happened to my office?"

"Elvis."

The name caused her chest to constrict. "What are you talking about?"

"The place is completely trashed. What isn't broken or shattered is burned."

"Burned?"

"All your files and stuff."

Barbara leaned against the wall. "Everything?"

"Everything in your office. The reception area was rifled through and the computer was smashed but—"

"Jeez, Dalton!" She listened for more than ten minutes as Dalton told her what had happened. When he was finished, he put Tracey back on the line. "What about the cartel stuff?"

"Gone," Tracey answered.

Barbara let out an expletive. "Look, I need your help. Can you come out here?"

"Sure," Tracey said. "I'll just leave my kids to fend for themselves. Child Services won't mind if I leave a three- and a five-year-old alone, and Lord knows I could use a vacation.''

"Sorry, I wasn't thinking," Barbara mumbled. "Okay, how about finding me a temp? Then call the supply place and have them ship me the stuff to re-create the storyboards.''

"Works for me. Where do you want it sent?''

"I'm at Cade Landry's ranch in Jasper, Montana.''

"You? At a ranch?" Tracey asked with a laugh.

"Please, just do it," Barbara directed. She glanced over at Cade and asked, "Is there a temp agency in Jasper?''

He shook his head as he took a sip of coffee. "He-lena has several.''

"Call Helena and have them send someone ASAP." Without covering the receiver, she asked Cade, "Do you have a computer I can use?''

He nodded. "I can get you one of the PC's from the cartel office.''

She shook her head. "I need state-of-the-art graph-ics programs." Into the telephone, she said, "When you call the temp agency, ask them to recommend a place where I can rent a computer, scanner and printer and send me our design and animation software.''

"Software's gone," Tracey said.

"Then order it from the supply place.''

"Consider it done. Anything else?''

"Go home.''

"What?''

"Take care of getting me set up out here while

Dalton's there, then go home. I don't want you anywhere near that place with Elvis running around.''

"I hate to break this to you, Barbara, but Elvis is dead. Has been since '77.''

"This isn't a joke, Tracey. Go home to your kids.''

"Full pay?''

Barbara had to smile. "Full pay.''

"Have fun down on the ranch.''

"Thanks.'' She hung up.

"Problems?'' Cade asked.

"Disasters,'' she answered. "Apparently, Elvis trashed my office and destroyed everything that wasn't nailed down.''

"Do they know why?'' Cade frowned as he leaned against the counter.

Barbara fell into a chair. "Because he could, according to Dalton. The police think he was looking for a way to locate me, and when he found nothing at the office, he left me a calling card.''

"Was anyone hurt?''

Barbara shook her head. "No, thank God. But the SOB destroyed all my work for the cartel. I'll have to redo everything.''

"Will that be possible?''

She nodded. "It'll take some time, though.''

"What size shoe do you wear?''

She blinked. "What?''

"Shoe size?''

"Six. Why?''

He nodded, apparently pleased. "You can wear a

pair of Jess's boots. She's a six and a half, but you can manage.''

''Why do I need boots?''

''I promised you a ride.''

She chuckled. ''And I said no thanks.''

''You don't have a choice. Mrs. Granger went into town for groceries and I have work to do before we go to the cartel offices this afternoon.''

''I'll stay here, thanks.''

''How's a cattleman supposed to trust you to handle his advertising if you've never seen a working cattle ranch up close?''

''I do ads for a gun-control group and I've never fired a gun. It's called imagination and creativity.''

''Look,'' he began as he buttoned his shirt, ''you have to redo all your ideas for the campaign, right?''

She nodded.

''Then think of this as research. You might find it inspiring.''

''Terrifying,'' she corrected.

''You'd risk taking on Elvis, but you won't sit a saddle?''

''Sit *in* a saddle,'' she corrected as if he were a small child.

''Shows what you know,'' he teased. ''We say 'sit a saddle' in this neck of the woods. You've got a lot to learn.''

''Why do you care?'' Barbara pressed. ''I'll be fine here.''

He shrugged and said, "Maybe it's my way of trying to make up for last night. Please?"

"I'LL NEED ROCK-CLIMBING gear to get all the way up there," Barbara gasped when the hand led a gray horse over to where they stood.

Cade laughed. "This is Darcy. She's as gentle as they come. Aren't you, girl?" He stroked the horse's long nose.

"I'll help you up, ma'am," the young man offered.

Cade gave T.J. a stern, silent warning. The kid was smart enough to back off. Too bad he wasn't smart enough to stop sniffing around Jess.

"I can't do this, Landry," Barbara said as she took a half step backward.

"Too late," he said, scooping her off the ground. He placed her in the saddle, keeping one hand at the small of her back. She squealed a little and sat perfectly stiff on the horse. "Relax."

"I will the instant you get me down."

"Put your feet in the stirrups and stop whining."

"I am not whining," she retorted with great hauteur. "I am scared witless. There is a difference."

"Good Lord, woman," he grumbled as he forced her foot into one stirrup. "Get a grip."

She pursed her lips, then said, "Go to hell."

A rumble of laughter passed through the hands assembled and watching from a safe distance. It wasn't safe enough. Cade turned, and that single action resulted in an immediate silence.

"If you're that afraid, we'll ride double."

"What's that?"

He looked up into her eyes. "I'll get up there with you. Of course, you'll have to hold on to me real tightlike and—"

"Pass, thanks," she interrupted.

Cade went to his own horse and mounted in one smooth, fluid motion. The animal adjusted to his weight, then stilled, waiting for Cade's command. He reined his horse next to hers and gave Barbara a brief lesson on guiding her animal.

A short time later, they were leisurely riding side by side. She didn't look as frightened, but he couldn't say she looked comfortable, either.

"How are you doing?"

"It isn't as bad as I thought," she admitted. "But I still resent the fact that you forced me to do this."

He wanted to laugh at her display of temper but thought better of it. Definitely not the right time to push any more of her buttons. He was still trying to figure out why he'd made her come with him in the first place. There was no way Elvis could find her, and even if he did, the Lazy L was secluded and secure.

Cade checked fencing and pointed out small landmarks as they rode. Barbara did little more than nod or mumble for the better part of a half hour. When they reached the west pass, he dismounted and tied his reins to a tree trunk. When he attempted to secure her horse to the same tree, she protested.

"If I get off, I won't get back on," she warned.

"If you don't take a break, your muscles will be screaming at you for days."

His fingers gripped her small waist as he helped her down. He kept holding her until she seemed steady. Somewhat reluctantly, he let go, went to his saddlebag and retrieved two bottles of water.

He turned to find Barbara leaning against a tree in order to stretch out her thighs. He waited a minute, then tossed her one of the bottles.

"I never would've thought cowboys went in for designer water," she teased.

Wearing a smile and a blush from the wind, she looked positively beautiful. Cade quickly averted his eyes. He didn't want to make another mistake in judgment. He needed Barbara here on the ranch.

"Tastes better," he shrugged as he pushed his hat back on his forehead. "I'll bet you only drink designer water, too."

"You'd be right," she agreed as she sat on a weathered rock. "Does the fact that I have money bother you for a reason, or just in general?"

Cade swallowed some water. "I have no problem with your net worth. I don't understand why you work when you don't have to."

"You aren't exactly poor, Landry. Would you be content sitting around on your tail all day?"

"Point taken," he answered with a smile. "Did you take over the family business?"

She let out a breath. "There was no family business. My father was a freelance merger and acquisition genius.''

''Was?''

''He died when I was in college.''

''Sorry.''

''He was a little bit like you,'' she commented starkly.

''I sense that wasn't a compliment.''

She didn't answer right away, apparently measuring her response. ''My father and I didn't get along very well.''

''A mama's girl?''

''My mother died when I was four,'' she told him. ''I don't even remember her.''

Cade kicked a pebble with the toe of his boot. ''I'm glad Jess knew her mother.''

''And she has doting grandparents if the car is any indication.''

Cade felt himself scowl. ''They're good people, but they don't seem able to say no to her.''

''Your daughter doesn't seem interested in taking no for an answer.''

He blew a breath toward the brim of his hat. ''I'm hoping this is just a phase.''

''It is,'' Barbara assured him.

He looked at her more intently. ''Was that encouragement, or were you being polite?''

''Truth. You just need to let her make her own mistakes.''

''I'm letting her keep the car.''

Barbara toyed with a lock of her hair. "What about T.J.?"

"He's an eighteen-year-old walking hormone. If he gets within ten yards of my kid, I'll kill him."

She laughed. "See? You're making him forbidden fruit."

"'Forbidden' being the operative word," he agreed.

"The more you tell her she can't see him, the more attractive he'll become."

"Did that happen to you?"

She shook her head. "The exact opposite. My father started scouting potential husbands for me when I reached puberty. Fortunately, I wasn't like him. I don't need a relationship to define myself."

"Sounds lonely."

She smiled, but it didn't reach her eyes. "I'm not lonely, Landry. I happen to have a very full life."

"Full of work."

She cast him a sidelong glance. "You must not have a very full social calendar since you were able to bring me here."

"I jumped into a relationship once. I won't make that mistake twice."

"Especially with your daughter running interference for you."

"Jess gets jealous."

"So did I. Funny," she said rather wistfully, "my father and I barely spoke a civil word to one another, but whenever he got serious about a woman, I sabotaged it.''

"Why?"

"I was young and stupid," she answered frankly. "Because of me, he never remarried."

"Did he want to?"

She nodded but kept her face hidden from him. "He used to tell me how great it had been between him and my mom. He wanted that again. He came close once, but I ruined it."

"How?"

"I told him that if he married the woman, I'd leave home."

"He should have tanned your hide."

"He knew I was serious."

"Were you?"

"Yes."

"So," Cade began cautiously as he approached her, "have you hated all men since then?"

"I don't hate men," she insisted, clearly affronted.

He smiled knowingly. "As long as they fit your safe definition of a man."

"What is that supposed to mean?"

"A hundred bucks says you only date polished wimps with expense accounts instead of spines. The kind of men who will bend to your every whim."

She got to her feet, glaring all the way. "I prefer to date *refined* men. Call me picky, but I happen to like men with manners."

"That's probably because you've never been with

the right man.'' He laughed, realizing he'd struck a nerve. "Hell, I bet you wouldn't even know what to do with a real man, Barbara. You're too afraid.''

"I'm not afraid of anything,'' she said as she planted her hands on her hips. "Men least of all.''

"Liar.''

"Jerk.''

"Chicken.''

"Bigger jerk.''

Cade removed his hat and placed it on his saddle, without ever breaking eye contact with her. "Prove it.''

"Prove what?'' Her blue eyes narrowed as her chin jutted with just the right amount of arrogance. "You think I'm afraid of you, Landry? Well, I'm not. I'm simply not interested.''

His smile was slow and purposeful. It took a great effort for him to keep his hands at his sides. He wanted to grab her and pull her against him. Kiss her until that superior mouth melted beneath his. "Yes, you are.'' He bent his head so his mouth was close to her ear. "I'd be more than happy to prove my point. Want to show me that I'm wrong, Barbara?''

Chapter Seven

So there was some truth to what he'd said, she acknowledged as she slipped into the claw-foot tub. She *was* interested, but Barbara would have swallowed her own tongue before she'd admit as much to Landry and his ego. All she wanted to do was get the smell of horse off her and some of the nagging stiffness from her muscles.

"Arrogant creep," she muttered like a mantra as she lathered and rinsed her hair. "How did I let myself get talked into this?"

She didn't answer. She couldn't. Not then and not all during the process of getting dressed. She yanked on her slacks, envisioning Landry's piercing eyes in the process. The man saw too much, and he was working his way under her skin. Normally, she could brush off a man's pass easily. Landry was just a man, so why did her knees feel weak just thinking about him?

The situation was intolerable. And unique. "I do not get stupid over men," she told her image in the mirror as she applied some mascara. "I refuse to let this one be an exception."

She ran her fingers over her hair until she was able to capture it into a barrette. She checked her reflection, and aside from the red mark on her neck courtesy of Elvis, she looked okay. She would have felt better in a business suit. There was something about a suit and heels that made her feel professional. It was hard to maintain an air of professionalism when she looked like a chic, urban soccer mom.

"I *am* losing my mind," she muttered. "I never think of myself as a mom. Soccer or otherwise. That isn't you, Barbara. Don't forget that."

"Forget what?" Cade asked as he stuck his head inside the crack in her door.

"You forgot to pack my work clothes," she lied.

"We're pretty casual here. I figured you wouldn't need any of that stuff."

"Gee, thanks."

Barbara walked toward the door but stopped dead when his hand snaked out. Rough, callused fingertips brushed the skin at her throat.

"It's healing well," Cade said.

She only nodded, afraid if she opened her mouth she'd scream, "Take me, big boy!" It wasn't fair for this man to have such an effect on her. *Distance. I definitely need to keep him at a safe distance.*

She shoved his hand aside and put on her game face. "I'm all set to see your offices."

"Then let's go."

She followed Cade downstairs and out to the waiting four-wheel drive. He started the car and drove in the opposite direction from the airstrip. To Barbara, it seemed to take an hour just to reach the iron arch at the end of the dusty driveway.

"How can you stand such isolation?" she asked as Cade tipped his hat to the two men standing at either side of the entrance. "And what are those two doing?"

"They make sure no one gets onto the ranch uninvited."

She didn't much care for the ominous tone or its implication. "C'mon, Landry. You can't believe Elvis would come all this way, do you?"

He shrugged, allowing one hand to drop from the steering wheel to the console between them. "You can never be too careful."

Barbara let out a frustrated breath and shifted in her seat to look at his profile. "At best, Elvis might know that I was working on the cartel account. Since all my communications were with Mr. Breck, there's absolutely no way he could guess that I'd be languishing on your ranch."

He cocked one brow. "Languishing?"

She felt her shoulders slump. "No offense meant, but in case you haven't noticed, I'm not exactly in my element."

"Maybe you should consider expanding your horizons."

"Maybe I should go back where I belong. Dalton said he could put me up in a safe house."

She watched as his grip tightened on the steering wheel. "As I recall, you weren't interested in a safe house."

"Can you blame me?" she countered. "The experience with my friend Claire taught me that I'm not very good at sitting idly by."

Cade cracked the window and cool, fresh air wafted through the car. "Dalton told me what you did. How could you have been fool enough to put yourself in that sort of danger?"

Anger seethed over her in a hot wave. "You don't know what you're taking about."

"According to Dalton," he argued in raised tones, "you defied the police and managed to damn near get yourself killed by some maniac."

"Did Dalton also mention that I was too late? That my caution and lack of decisiveness probably got Claire killed? If I'd have acted a few hours sooner, she'd probably be alive."

"Or you'd be dead, too. What possessed a basically intelligent woman to do something so scatterbrained? I hear you almost got Dalton's wife killed, as well."

Barbara would have enjoyed slugging him at that moment. "You couldn't possibly understand. It wasn't your friend who was missing."

"No," he answered in a more subdued tone. "My friend was killed before my eyes."

Damn him for making me feel guilty! she thought.

"Okay, so maybe you understand part of it. But I'm not like you, Landry. I couldn't do nothing. I couldn't leave it to the police. Claire was like a sister to me."

"We're not as unalike as you think," he said, then fell silent for the remainder of the trip.

The cartel office was a nondescript, single-story building at the edge of what looked like a small commercial center. Had it not been for the blue-and-white sign welcoming her to Jasper, she probably wouldn't have known she was near a town.

She followed Cade to the building, taking in her surroundings as he flipped switches that caused fluorescent lights to flicker to life. The stale smell of cigar smoke hung in the air. Stacks of leaflets were everywhere, covering two long tables as well as a large portion of the desk. Cade went directly to an answering machine and pressed the button.

She quietly looked at the posters and photographs on the walls. It was an odd collection of pro-beef propaganda and family-style pictures. She walked toward a group photo hanging behind the desk. Immediately, she recognized Cade and Breck as well as five of the other eight men. They had all been at the Rose Tattoo the night of the shooting. They looked happy, more like fraternity brothers than a professional lobbying organization.

"This is Thomas Shelton."

Barbara's attention was piqued when she heard her competitor's voice on the answering-machine tape.

"I was sorry to hear about what happened in

Charleston," Shelton's voice continued. "Unless I hear differently, I'm still planning on coming at the end of the week. Please have someone call my office with the funeral arrangements. I'd like to be there to pay my respects to Dale. He was a hell of a good guy."

And you're a hell of a brownnoser, Barbara thought cattily.

Cade listened to an additional series of concerned phone calls from an assortment of men expressing outrage and condolences. All the while, he'd been ripping into the stack of mail and separating the correspondence into piles. The final message was from someone named Becky, asking to be called about the funeral and to be told when and if Cade wanted her to resume her duties at the office.

"I'll call Becky eventually," he said absently. "Since I don't see myself jumping right in here, why don't you see if this computer has anything you can use for your work."

"Is it worth it?" she asked, careful to keep her tone soft.

He gave her a questioning look. "What?"

She took a fortifying breath. "If Dale had already made arrangements for Thomas Shelton to—"

"I told you I'd give you a fair shake," he cut in curtly. "Check out the computer or not—your choice."

Barbara slipped past him and went to the desk. In under a minute, she had the machine's hard drive spinning to life. Ten minutes later, she was pretty sure the computer lacked the speed and drive space she would need in order to bring life to her ideas.

"I need more power," she told him as she began to scan the machine's contents to see if anything could be transferred to disks to free up some space. "I could off-load both of the correspondence folders, then restore them when I'm finished if no one will need them right away."

Cade came up behind her and began reading the list of files in the directory. His upper torso was pressed against her back and the scent of his soap teased her senses. It was difficult to focus on the words on the screen when every inch of her body tingled where it touched his. She had two choices. She could either jump out of the chair, which would let him know that his mere proximity was enough to make her crazy. Or she could pretend it didn't faze her that she could feel the outline of taut muscle.

Or, the dirty little part of her mind suggested, *I could shove everything off the desk, throw him down and ravish him until I get this absurd obsession out of my system.*

"This is incredible," Cade murmured close to her ear.

"Mmm."

He reached around her with strong arms, and just when she thought her wild fantasy had been telepathically communicated, his blunt-tipped fingers danced across the keyboard instead of her heated, needy skin.

Obviously, they defined *incredible* differently.
"What's wrong?"

Cade's deft maneuvering of the computer brought
up an accounting program that immediately denied
him access without a password. He cursed.

She brushed his hands away. "What was Mr.
Breck's birth date?"

"July 29, 1940."

Barbara tried the date in various combinations, including backward. Nothing. "Anniversary?" Cade
thought for a minute and gave her a second date. It,
too, was useless. They tried Dale's social security
number, his age, his telephone number, his home address, and still nothing. "What about his wife?"

"She died, remember."

"When?"

Cade raked his hands through his hair, then said,
"September 15, 1991."

Barbara typed 09151991 and the screen flashed
"HELLO DALE" in large blue letters.

"Very good," Cade said with enough sincerity to
make her feel like a giddy teenager. "Were you a
hacker in another life?"

She laughed. "Nope. I just read someplace that the
most common passwords are dates with special mean-
ings. People tend not to forget them as easily."

She scrolled down through the entries. It didn't
take long for her to realize that she was looking at a
personal checking account. One that was seriously
overdrawn until one week earlier.

"That's a hefty deposit," Barbara noted. Glancing over her shoulder, she saw that Cade's expression was troubled. "I didn't realize selling cattle was so lucrative," she added as she read the description beneath the entry. "How many cows do you have to sell to earn twenty-five thousand dollars in one shot?"

"More head than Dale ran."

"I don't understand," she said. "Was he selling those things—what are they called—futures?"

Cade shook his head. "Dale sold off most of his herd after his wife died. He divided up a good portion of his land for residential development."

"You're losing me, Landry. Are you telling me that Dale Breck didn't have anything worth twenty-five thousand to sell?"

"Not that I know of." He reached past her and picked up the phone, pressing buttons in rapid fashion.

"Are you calling Dalton?"

He shook his head. "My cousin Seth."

"Why?"

He waved her off and gave the call his complete attention. "Seth, it's Cade.... Yeah, thanks. I need a favor. Can you call a detective in Charleston and do whatever's necessary to get your hands on Dale's bank records for the week before he was killed?" There was a brief pause before he said, "Thanks. Have the stuff sent out to my place." He provided his cousin with Dalton's name and number, then hung up. Without missing a beat, he placed his hand on her shoulder and asked, "Can you see if the cartel's financial records are on here?"

It took Barbara less than a minute. "They look fine. Nothing but printers, suppliers, reimbursements."

Cade cursed again, then picked up a coffee mug from the edge of the desk and sent it flying across the room. His eyes glistened with pent-up rage.

"Calm down, Cade. Tell me what's wrong?"

"I don't recognize half those entries. I sure as hell didn't sign off on the checks. All disbursements required my signature as well as Dale's."

Barbara began to work her way through the current partial year's activities. "It isn't like the account is empty," she said. "The cartel has almost fifty thousand dollars in it."

"It should have twice that," he barked. "I can't believe Dale was stealing from us. God, what a mess."

"Hold on," Barbara said as she placed her hand on his upper arm. "Maybe Dale was just a lousy bookkeeper. You're in charge now, right?"

He nodded.

"Then why don't we go to the bank and get copies of everything."

Cade held her gaze. "He was my friend. Hell, he was like a father to me."

"Then give him the benefit of the doubt," she urged. "Maybe it's sloppy record keeping. If not, maybe Dale was spending the money legitimately. Don't condemn him until you have all the facts."

Some of the anger seemed to drain from his eyes. He offered a weak smile. "I got the impression you didn't like Dale."

"I didn't know him," Barbara said. "But if the worst turns out to be true, it might explain why Elvis killed him."

Chapter Eight

Jasper, she soon learned, consisted of a dozen or so organized streets with modest Victorian homes sharing tree-lined blocks with small businesses. Not unlike Charleston, there were hitching posts at some curbs. Unlike her hometown, these hitching posts were still utilized.

Cade drove over a small bridge above a swift-moving stream into the parking lot of a place called the Mountainview Inn. It was a beautiful log building with grand windows and landscaped pathways on either side.

"What are we doing here?" she asked.

"I'm going to leave you in the restaurant while I run a few errands." Cade's announcement was followed by a quick exit from the car.

Barbara tried to remind herself that he had just learned some potentially incriminating information about a close friend, but she'd be damned before she'd be dropped off like a bag of laundry.

"Hold on!" She grabbed his arm, but it didn't impede his departure. "Landry, wait, please?"

He stopped abruptly, which caused Barbara to stumble into him. He steadied her with strong hands. "What?"

"I want to know why you're dumping me here. I'm the one who got you into the computer system in the first place."

He glared at her with such fierceness that she actually stepped back. "I've got things to do and I don't want you around right now."

Pure wrath surged through her veins. "I don't want to be around you right now, either. But I don't want to sit in some restaurant."

His jaw tightened and his eyes narrowed dangerously. "I'm not in any mood to be pushed right now, Barbara, so do as I say."

She glared right back at him. She was so involved in their silent clash that she barely noticed the patrol car pulling in.

"Trouble?" the officer asked as he strolled over with an annoying smile on his face.

"This jerk is threatening me," Barbara said without really looking at the man. "I'd like to have him arrested. He's a menace."

"You're the menace," Cade fired back.

To her dismay, the officer began to laugh. She turned her anger on him. "You think it's funny for a man to threaten a woman? What kind of lame excuse for a policeman are you?"

The man touched the rim of his hat with deference. "I'm the sheriff, ma'am. Seth Landry."

Barbara threw her hands in the air with utter exasperation. "Great! I forgot the authority figure around here is a relative."

"What'd you do to her, Cade?" the sheriff asked, clearly amused. "You sure got her dander up."

"I do not have dander," Barbara said between clenched teeth. "And please refrain from speaking about me as if I were invisible."

Seth's dark brows arched as he gave her a slow perusal. "No, ma'am. You certainly aren't invisible."

"Watch it," Cade warned.

"Don't you dare make some pathetic attempt at defending my honor, Landry. And you..." She glared at what passed for law enforcement. "Are you going to do your sworn duty or are you going to keep checking me out like some low-life barfly?"

Seth whistled. "Got yourself a spirited one, Cade."

Barbara squeezed her eyes shut and silently prayed for patience, secretly hoping that a bolt of lightning would zap the both of them. "That's it," she announced. "I've had all of this I care to take. Forget the account, Landry. It isn't worth putting up with all this!"

She got exactly one and a half steps before Cade's arm snaked around her waist and he snatched her off the ground. She spit a rather lengthy list of unflattering names at him.

"Calm down!" he ordered.

"Then put me down!" Her attempts to kick his shins were easily and expertly avoided.

"Um, Cade," she heard Seth begin, "careful you don't hurt her."

Barbara almost screamed but wasn't willing to give Cade the satisfaction.

"I'm not going to hurt her. I'm just trying to get her to go inside and wait for me."

"When hell freezes over," Barbara assured him testily.

"How about I take her off your hands?" the sheriff offered.

Barbara swung her head in his direction. "How about the two of you take a flying leap?"

The radio on the sheriff's shoulder crackled to life. A woman's voice said, "Seth, you there?"

Cade kept hold of her while Seth spoke into the mouthpiece. "I'm here, Myrtle. Whatcha need?"

"We got a call from the Lazy L. They're looking for Cade."

"He's here. What's the problem?"

"That girl of his."

Cade's grip loosened and Barbara was gently lowered to the ground. "What?"

"Seems she's out on the edge of Highway 7."

"Doing what?" Seth asked.

"Asking for a tow to get that fancy new car of hers out of the ditch she drove it into."

Cade swore and pulled Barbara back toward the car.

"DADDY! DON'T!"

Cade's fist connected with the young man's chin with less than half the force he knew he was capable of using. Still, the blow sent T.J. sprawling onto the ground. "Get up."

"You aren't solving anything," Barbara said as she stepped between him and his target. "You're twice his size and you're supposed to be the adult."

"I'm three times your size," he warned as he met her insolent gaze. "But that doesn't mean I'll hurt you."

As usual, Barbara obviously refused to be intimidated by him. She remained toe-to-toe, glaring up at him with fire in her eyes.

When she reached out and touched a tentative hand to his sleeve, Cade felt some of his anger begin to drain. Odd that just the hint of her touch should so easily calm him.

"He's only eighteen," Barbara said. "She's only sixteen and you aren't going to accomplish anything by using brute force."

He let out an exasperated breath as he looked from the ditched car to Jess, then back to Barbara. "She could've killed herself."

Her expression seemed to soften. "But she didn't. So I suggest we all go back to the house and discuss this like rational people."

"I don't need *her* to defend me," Jess whined.

Before Cade could counsel his daughter, Barbara

faced her and said, "You're right. Your actions aren't defensible. You broke your father's trust."

For the first time he could remember in a long while, Jess was rendered speechless by Barbara's calmly delivered rebuke.

Cade ordered T.J. to wait with the car while he took Jess and Barbara back to the house. His bad day was getting worse and his mood wasn't improved when he spotted a strange woman sitting on his front steps.

"Great," he muttered as he threw the car into Park behind a small compact car he guessed belonged to the woman. He thought the tall, primly dressed brunette was some sort of salesperson, probably a rep for one of the equipment companies that supplied the ranch.

Jess bounded from the car and made a beeline for the door, passing the woman as she took the steps two at a time.

"Hello," the woman greeted as she rose, holding tightly to a thin black briefcase. "I'm—"

"Now isn't a good time," Cade interrupted. "In the future, make an appointment with Slick Drummond."

"B-but," she stammered, "I'm Olivia Miles from Helena Helpers."

Cade mumbled an apology. "You want to talk to her," he said as he nodded his head in Barbara's direction.

"You must be Miss Prather," Olivia said with a

broad smile. "I was told to come as soon as possible."

He watched as Barbara gave the woman a firm handshake. "Thank you, Olivia. I've got to talk to Mr. Landry for a few minutes." She looked at Cade and asked, "Is there someplace she can wait?"

He shrugged. "Sure. I'll have Jess see to it."

Jess was more than willing to get the temp a drink and keep her company while he was forced to endure whatever lecture Barbara had planned for him. Cade knew Jess was only doing it to try to earn points with him. He didn't bother to tell her that it didn't matter. He wasn't about to overlook the fact that she had disobeyed him. He couldn't. Her safety depended on her staying in Helena for now.

With Jess and the temp settled in the kitchen, he called down to the barn and instructed two of his hands to take the truck down to the highway to retrieve the car and T.J. With just a touch of residual malice, he told them to take their time getting there.

He could tell by the pensive look on Barbara's pretty face that he was in for another one of her parenting lectures. Cade went to his study and took the seat behind his desk. His eyes followed her as she checked out the room. When she finally took one of the high-backed chairs opposite the desk, he was again struck by how small she was. No, not small—petite, delicate. And very, very feminine. Instead of harboring his anger, he found his thoughts going in a decidedly different direction. Silently, he admired the regal way she held her head. The chair became a throne with her in it and he felt like her humble subject instead of the king of his own domain. The woman had a real knack for throwing him off-kilter.

"Make it quick," he said in his most detached voice.

Her pale eyebrows drew together as she stared at him intently. When she took a fortifying breath, Cade noticed the way her blouse pulled taut against the outline of her breasts. No matter how much he willed himself not to notice, he couldn't seem to help it. Even when she donned her professional mask, he was keenly aware of her subtle sensuality. A sensuality he doubted she acknowledged.

Barbara seemed unaware of the fact that her pursed lips made him wonder what it would be like to kiss her. Did she know that a few strands of hair had fallen free of her barrette? Could she sense how he longed to see her hair tumble to her shoulders?

"You overreacted," she stated simply.

"Well, the way I see it, that's my job as a father."

"Punching a defenseless kid?"

Cade laughed without amusement. "He isn't defenseless, and legally, he's a man."

"Did you bother to ask what he was doing with your daughter?" she challenged.

He rolled his eyes. "I didn't need to ask. Jess has made it perfectly clear that she—"

"My point exactly," Barbara cut in as she rose. "If you'd open your stubborn eyes, you'd see that it's

Jessica who's doing the pursuing.'' She came around the desk and half sat on the edge so that they were at eye level. ''I know you're upset by the stuff you found at the office today, but you shouldn't let that cloud your judgment.''

''What's clouded about finding my daughter on a deserted stretch of road with one of my ranch hands?''

She leaned forward slightly. ''Did you ever consider the possibility that your daughter invited him for a ride in her new toy? You acted as if you found them naked instead of simply sitting on the side of the road. And what about the other possibility that T.J. is smart enough not to grope his boss's daughter in broad daylight?''

''They ran the car into a ditch,'' he shot back. ''Why do you think she lost control of the car?''

''She's probably a lousy driver,'' Barbara reasoned. ''If you'd have taken a look at the road instead of coming out swinging, you might have noticed the skid marks.''

''Skid marks?''

Barbara nodded. ''She was clearly over the center line when she hit the brakes. My guess is she was going too fast and simply lost control. Why don't you *ask* her what happened instead of assuming?''

''You can't really be that naive,'' Cade argued.

''I'm not naive,'' she assured him. ''I just don't think you have enough facts to conclude the two of them were…well…'' She seemed flustered for a second, then finished by saying, "Were doing anything other than driving."

Cade snorted and raked his fingers through his hair. "I'm starting to think you have no clue about the chemistry between the male and female of the species."

Faint color appeared on her cheeks. "Don't be condescending, Landry. You're the one who doesn't have a clue. Males and females can be in close proximity without resorting to sexual contact."

He couldn't help but smile. "You're deluding yourself, Miss Prather. Whenever men and women are alone together, there is always an undercurrent. It's a simple fact of life."

She made a dismissive little noise. "We're not talking about a woman, Landry. We were talking about a sixteen-year-old girl."

Intentionally, he leaned forward and lowered his voice. "Maybe I'm changing the subject."

A flash of exasperation narrowed her eyes. "Well, I'm not."

She started to move, but he placed his hands on either side of her, trapping her there. His gaze locked on hers. "Humor me, Barbara."

The exasperation evolved into something new. Something he couldn't decipher. At first, he thought her big blue eyes were communicating trepidation, but he wasn't sure. Hell, lately he wasn't sure of much. And he didn't like it.

"Humor you how?"

"Honesty," he answered quietly.

She seemed uneasy. It was as if that one word had made a chink in the protective armor of aloofness she used as a shield. He'd seen it twice before. The first time was when Dale was shot. Barbara's cool exterior had cracked in the horror and chaos of that moment. It had happened again at her apartment. Without realizing it, she'd shown him her soft, vulnerable side after Elvis had attacked her.

"Why are you afraid of me?" he asked.

She attempted a brave smile. "Afraid? Hardly. I'm angry that you've resorted to these tactics again."

Slowly, Cade lifted his hands away from the desk, giving her total freedom to stay or leave. His eyes never left her face. "I'm not trying to make you angry."

Her head tilted to one side. "Then what are you trying to do?"

He moved his hands over so that his palms rested atop her thighs. He felt her muscles tense beneath his touch. "I'm not sure what I'm trying to do," he told her.

Her mouth drew into a tight line. "You've got your hands on me after I've repeatedly told you not to do that."

He nodded. "I know. I can't seem to help myself."

She drew her lower lip between her teeth and her gaze never faltered. "I—I don't want this."

He looked at her for no more than a minute but it felt like an eternity. "Because of the account?"

She gave a quick nod. "It isn't ethical, Cade. You're a potential client, and I—"

"What if I wasn't?"

She blinked. "But you are."

"If I wasn't?" he pressed as his fingers began to gently explore the contours of her legs.

He heard a small catch in her breath. "But you are."

A smile slowly formed on his lips. "Does that mean I have a shot after I consider your presentation?"

Barbara reached down and stilled his hands. "No. I'm not going to let this happen."

Somehow her eyes and her words seemed at odds. "Maybe I can change your mind."

"Obviously, you could do that rather easily. But it would be a huge mistake."

"Excuse me?"

Lifting his hands away, she carefully placed them back on the desk. "You're a handsome, virile, sexy man, Landry, but you already know that. You want honesty? Okay. I'll admit that for some unknown reason, I'm attracted to you—"

"That's a start."

"But," she continued as she slipped off the desk, "I won't jeopardize my professional reputation and my personal ethics."

"I wouldn't ask you to."

"No," she said with a heavy sadness, "you

wouldn't. But there's no practical way things could work out between us.''

He caught her chin between his thumb and forefinger. ''It isn't supposed to be practical, Barbara. It's about passion.''

Her smile was weak but genuine. ''Passion is fleeting, Landry.''

''It doesn't have to be.''

''AND I HAVE EXPERIENCE in using all kinds of software,'' Olivia was saying.

Barbara forced herself to focus on the résumé the woman had provided. Judging by her credentials, she was perfect. ''I'll need you to graph and chart demographics for me in presentation format. I'm having equipment delivered tomorrow, so we can get started then.''

Olivia nodded, her dark eyes fixed and expressionless. She acted more like a robot than a person, but Barbara didn't care. In fact, Olivia's no-nonsense style would definitely be an asset if she was going to pull everything together in a short period of time.

''If it will help, I can go to the library tonight and access information on buying trends and potential beef consumers,'' Olivia offered.

Barbara wanted to hug the woman. ''That would be a huge help. I should've thought of that myself.''

''No problem. I'll get started, and if you need additional figures, I can get them off the Internet once you have a system in place here.''

Barbara offered her another cup of coffee, which she declined. "I've already had too much," she said. "I'm sorry if I arrived early. The agency said to come right away."

"*I'm* sorry I kept you waiting for so long," Barbara countered with a smile.

"Mr. Landry's daughter showed me around the house. It was no problem, really." Olivia stood, then reached into her briefcase and pulled out a piece of paper. "This is my home number if you need to reach me before morning."

"I really appreciate it," Barbara said as she led the woman toward the front door. "I know this place is rather out of the way. I'd be happy to reimburse you for mileage or other expenses."

"Thank you, but it isn't necessary. I'm looking forward to working out here. It's very peaceful, isn't it?"

Barbara considered the comment and found herself agreeing. "A little isolated for me, though." She walked Olivia to her car.

"I suppose it is," she said. "But isn't that better than the frantic pace of a big city?"

"You aren't a native here?"

The woman fumbled for the single key on her chain. "No. I grew up all over. I'll be here at nine tomorrow."

"See you then."

Barbara rubbed her arms as she climbed the front steps. The late-afternoon air held a chill in spite of the fact that summer was just weeks away. Olivia's presence was going to make her job a lot easier. Since Cade was making her life extremely difficult, that would be a big help.

She suddenly didn't want to risk running into him. His little comment about passion still haunted her thoughts. Turning abruptly, she began to walk in the direction of the corral. She was only vaguely aware that her presence attracted the attention of the dozen or so men working at various jobs. Picking up her pace, she stared at the majestic mountains in the distance. Snow blanketed the summits and she found herself wondering what it would be like to see the world from way up there. She smiled. She had similar thoughts at home whenever she stared out at the Atlantic Ocean. Finding a parallel between her world and Cade's was alternately comforting and disconcerting.

"Hey!"

She turned at the sound of Jessica's voice. The girl was a few yards behind her, jogging to close the distance.

"I like Barbara better than 'hey,'" she said.

Jess eyed her cautiously with lingering belligerence in her expression. "Dinner will be ready in a half hour. My dad said I should get you."

"Okay."

The two of them walked about a quarter mile in silence until Jessica finally spoke. "Daddy's sending me back to Helena again."

"Really?"

Jessica walked more slowly. "How come you stuck up for T.J. today?"

"Because I didn't think he deserved to be punched."

"He didn't," Jessica admitted in a childish pout. "I was only showing him the car. We weren't doing anything wrong."

"Did you explain that to your father?"

"I tried, but Daddy just kept yelling at me for coming back out here after he told me to stay in Helena."

"You disobeyed him. I'm sure he'll get over it."

"The car is fine except for one scratch," she said. "But T.J. won't even look at me now."

"Maybe that's for the best," Barbara suggested.

"That's *so* not true," Jessica wailed. "I'm in love with T.J. and it's not fair of Daddy to keep us apart."

"What about T.J.?"

She watched as the girl's shoulders slumped slightly. "I know he'd fall in love with me if we just spent some time together. I'll just die if Daddy doesn't lighten up some. You have no idea what it's like to have someone trying to run your whole life. It isn't fair!"

"Maybe you should be glad you're only a few hours away. My father sent me to Switzerland when I was your age."

"No lie?" Jessica gasped. "What'd you do to deserve that?"

Barbara smiled. "I developed a huge crush on my father's driver."

Jessica let out a sigh. "Was he hot?"

Barbara bit the inside of her cheek to keep from laughing. "Very. I spent the first six months being sure he would come for me."

"Did he?"

Now she did laugh. "No. Apparently, he'd gotten some girl pregnant, and by the time I came home for the Christmas break, he was married."

"Were you crushed?"

"Sure."

"What did you do?"

"Nothing."

"Why not?"

"I don't know. One day I woke up and realized what I would've given up if I'd been the one who got pregnant and married at sixteen."

"I want a family," Jessica said fiercely.

"Nothing wrong with that," Barbara commented.

"Then how come you didn't have one when you were young?"

"Ouch," Barbara grumbled. "I'm not that old, Jessica."

"Whatever." Jessica began to jog ahead. "Don't be late for dinner again. It really yanks Mrs. Granger's chain."

Luckily, Barbara was able to avoid any sign of Cade as she made her way to her room. She slipped inside and replayed her conversation with Jessica. At least it had been civil. That was a start.

Start? her brain repeated. *I'm here to win the cartel's account, not the trust of Landry's daughter.*

Barbara opened the closet to retrieve a sweater and saw the contents of her purse strewn on the floor. She knelt and began replacing things but soon realized that certain items had been disturbed. For starters, the rubber band was off her personal address book.

Anger pounded in her head. No wonder Jessica had tried to make nice. The little snot had obviously violated her privacy. Glancing up at her clothes, Barbara noted that many were hanging askew on the hangers. Next she checked the drawers, which also showed signs of rifling. Gently, she kicked the bedpost, thinking herself a fool for being taken in by a sixteen-year-old.

Chapter Nine

"Is she gone?"

Cade looked up from the stack of documents that had been delivered just after dinner. Barbara was wearing the same unreadable look she'd had all through the early part of the evening.

"Jess is on her way back to Helena and I've called my former in-laws and threatened them if they don't keep closer tabs on that girl." He tossed the red pen he'd been using onto the desk and rubbed his strained eyes. "It's worse than I thought."

"You could say that," Barbara agreed wryly. "Did she tell you?"

Letting out a breath, he looked with disgust at the bank records Seth had gotten for him. "I didn't talk to anyone at the bank. Not that I need to. Dale was skimming from the cartel account for years."

Her expression seemed to soften as she came around the desk and peered over his shoulder. He could hear the faint, soothing sounds of each breath as she silently reviewed the copies. "This was going on for five years?" she asked.

He nodded through the thick blanket of betrayal. "I've been cross-referencing the cartel accounts with Dale's personal account and he was transferring cartel money to himself. Then on the fifteenth of every month, he wrote a check to Montana Rentals."

"Maybe there's some explanation, Cade. Dale might've had a reason for paying that company by personal check rather than a cartel check."

He looked up into her soft blue eyes. "Montana Rentals is a small business center between Jasper and Helena. They rent post-office boxes and sell money orders." He watched and waited as she absorbed the meaning of his statement. "I called and inquired. All they would tell me is that Dale was a customer."

"I'm sure Dalton can—"

"Already called him," Cade said. "He told me he'll work on it through legal channels, but it could take a while. He said something about an out-of-state warrant."

She offered an encouraging smile. "I'm sure it isn't great to learn that your friend was stealing, but you may have found the clue that will lead to solving his murder."

"The Charleston M.E. is releasing his body tomorrow." Cade blew out a breath. "How am I supposed to deliver his eulogy when I've just found out he's been screwing us all over for years? If he was having money problems, why didn't he come to me? I would've helped him out."

He closed his eyes but only for an instant. They flew open when he felt the brush of her body against his. The chair squeaked slightly as she wriggled between him and the desk. Her hands rested on his shoulders and Cade was afraid to move. He was more afraid not to.

"You may never get the answers you want," she said softly. "Keep your focus on the Dale you knew, not the one you never met."

As if it was the most natural thing in the world, Cade slipped his arms around her tiny waist, lacing his fingers at the small of her back. "Right now, I'd like to forget about this whole mess."

She nodded and started to pull away. "I'm not here as a diversion," she cautioned.

He kept hold of her and met her level gaze. "I know that, Barbara." Standing, he pulled her against him, backing her against the edge of the desk. Slowly, his hands rose to cup her beautiful face in his palms. She swallowed and he prepared himself for rejection. He was caught in limbo as he savored the floral scent of her hair and the smooth heat of her skin. Breath, warm and urgent, spilled through her slightly parted lips. He told himself he shouldn't kiss her. It wasn't what she wanted. But it *was* the only thing he wanted.

Straining against his own need, he allowed his lips to touch hers, hoping that would be enough. Knowing instantly it was only a beginning. Her hands flattened against his chest, just above his urgently beating heart. He applied pressure until her mouth willingly opened beneath his.

He hesitated only long enough to breathe in the taste of her. His thumbs teased the line of her jaw as he forced her back until she was nearly flat on the desk. His tongue tested her upper lip. A soft moan rumbled in her throat as he deepened the kiss.

He wasn't even sure it was a kiss. That single word seemed too simple a description for the torrent of desire surging through him. Abandoning any pretext, Cade wound one hand through her thick hair while the other touched her cheek, then dipped in a sensual exploration of her neck. Barbara's hands moved around him, urging him closer still. She tasted as hot and wild as he felt. Her response very nearly robbed him of what little self-control remained.

He ran his hand along her side. Traced the generous swell of her breast, the outline of her ribs, the gentle slope of her hip. He was only vaguely aware of the low rumbles of arousal in his own throat as he reached for the top of her blouse.

His fingers were fumbling with the first small button when she drew his lip into her mouth and bit him gently. He hadn't been prepared for the mind-jolting thrill of her aggression. Without meaning to, he pulled on her blouse and heard the soft ping of buttons scattering on the desk, then falling to the floor.

He aligned his mouth with hers as his hand closed over the firmness of her breast. She gasped into his mouth when his thumb dipped beneath the lace of her bra to touch her taut nipple. It was pure heaven when she arched against him. Cade felt every inch of her and he was sure she felt every inch of him. The sheer power of the encounter was all-consuming. Whatever he'd imagined, it paled badly in the reality of having her beneath him.

Blood pounded in his head. His ears. *No,* his mind registered through the fog of his desire. It wasn't blood pounding. It was someone knocking on the door frame.

Lifting his head, he realized that his housekeeper was discreetly standing in the shadows of the open door. "What?" he demanded in a voice that conveyed his frustration.

"Er...there's a gentleman here to see you," Mrs. Granger said.

"Tell him to go away," Cade ordered, but he knew the moment had passed.

Barbara was shoving him off her. She looked at him with imploring eyes that still held traces of unspent passion. Whoever was at the door was a dead man.

"He says he has an appointment with you," Mrs. Granger said with obvious discomfort in her voice. "A Mr. Shelton."

Cade heard Barbara's strangled curse as she scurried away from him. He caught only a fleeting glance of cleavage and lace before she captured the edges of her torn blouse in a stranglehold.

"This is great!" she cried as she took in deep breaths.

"Calm down," Cade instructed as he attempted to regain control of his own breathing. "I'll show him into the kitchen. He won't even see you." He hated the guilty look in her eyes. "You don't have to look like I just killed your dog," he teased.

She glared at him. "If you tell Shelton that——"

Ire raced through him. "Don't worry, Barbara. I may not be one of your cultured, well-mannered whipping boys, but I am decent enough to keep private matters private."

He stormed out of the room, slamming the door behind him.

BARBARA SPENT five minutes changing her clothes and thirty minutes hiding. The problem was, she couldn't hide from herself. Kissing Cade had been a huge mistake.

It had also been the single most thrilling experience of her life.

She touched her fingers to her mouth, relishing the memory. In all her years, she had never been kissed with such raw desire. There was nothing polished or practiced about the way Cade had ravished her mouth or her senses. She'd never felt so needed, so desired. It was so primal it was almost animalistic in its power.

"It was also incredibly stupid," she whispered as she forced herself toward the door. "Never mix business and pleasure." *Even if it is the most extraordinary pleasure known to mankind.*

The sounds of Thomas Shelton and Cade sharing a laugh rankled. Here she was a walking bundle of quivering nerve endings and they were doing some serious male bonding. Still, she wanted to make her presence known. Let Shelton realize that she intended to go after the account as single-mindedly as he did.

To his credit, Shelton didn't look at her with accusation. In fact, he seemed to think that finding her in Landry's home was natural and normal.

"Barbara, you remember Thomas Shelton," Cade said as he stood and pulled out one of the kitchen chairs for her.

Accepting the chair, Barbara sat at the round oak table, careful not to make eye contact with Cade. She wanted to make a point to Shelton, but she knew that wouldn't happen if she started blushing like a teenager.

"Nice to see you again, Mr. Shelton," she said as she sized him up. He was giving her an easy smile that didn't seem to reach his blue eyes. His suit was off-the-rack and his shoes were knockoffs. It hardly fitted the image he'd given her the night of the party. She'd been led to believe that Shelton was the latest whiz kid out of New York.

"You look lovely, Miss Prather. Montana obviously agrees with you," he said smoothly.

Too smoothly. "I was under the impression that

you weren't coming out here until the end of the week.''

He nodded. Thanks to mousse, not a single red hair moved in the process. ''When I heard that Mr. Breck's body was being returned, I decided to come out early to see if I could assist with the funeral.''

''How nice,'' Barbara said. She then looked over toward the cabinet and saw a portfolio resting there. ''Your presentation?'' she asked.

He gave her an ''Aw, shucks, you caught me'' shrug. ''I'm superstitious. I didn't want to risk leaving it back at my hotel room. You never know when things will accidentally get destroyed or misplaced.''

She kept her smile in place. ''Don't be coy, Mr. Shelton. You obviously know that my office was broken into.''

He offered a less than apologetic expression. ''My friend in Charleston did mention it to me when he told me about Mr. Breck.''

''Who is your friend?'' she asked. ''Perhaps I know him.''

''I doubt that,'' Shelton replied. ''He's a friend from college.''

''Really? Where did you go to college?''

''In your backyard, Miss Prather,'' Shelton answered. ''College of Charleston.''

Cade rose and returned with the coffeepot and a mug for Barbara. ''Small world, huh?'' Cade remarked.

''Very small,'' Barbara agreed. ''My father endowed a scholarship there. I've continued the tradition."

Shelton's grin widened. "You're philanthropic as well as talented."

"You have me at a disadvantage, Mr. Shelton. I'm not familiar with any of your work."

Shelton covered his coffee cup and stood. "No more for me, thanks," he said to Cade. "I need to be getting back to the Mountainview Inn. It's a long drive and I've already intruded on you and your guest long enough."

Cade extended his hand. "I'll see you tomorrow at the cartel office."

"Thank you." Shelton nodded his head at Barbara. "Miss Prather."

Hugging the cup in both hands, she remained in the kitchen while Cade showed Shelton to the door.

"Are you always so guarded around the competition?" Cade asked when he returned. "Or are you still feeling guilty because of what happened in the study?"

Heat splashed on her cheeks. "Don't go there, Landry."

He moved over to the counter and leaned back, crossing his ankles and pinning her with his gaze. "Am I supposed to pretend it didn't happen?"

"Works for me."

"No way," he told her.

"Please," she pleaded. "It was an error in judgment. It shouldn't have happened. I shouldn't have let it happen. I'm willing to take full responsibility for letting it happen, but…'' Her voice trailed off when she read the amusement in his eyes. "You think this is funny?''

"Yep.''

Irritation grated on her frazzled nerves. "It was a mistake and it won't happen again.''

"Yes, it will,'' he told her, punctuating his answer with a wink. "And soon.''

Barbara pressed her lips together for a moment to contain her temper. "Cocky is unattractive and unappealing in a man, Landry.''

"I'm not being cocky. I'm being honest.''

"So am I,'' she assured him. "I don't want you to kiss me again.''

He shrugged. "Fine.''

She regarded him with caution. "That was too easy.''

"You don't want me to kiss you again, I won't kiss you again.''

"Th-thank you for respecting my wishes.''

He gave her his best lopsided grin. "I don't need to kiss you again.''

Barbara should have felt relief. Instead, she felt…stinging rejection. "Fine.''

Cade laughed softly. "I won't need to kiss you…'' he began as he came over to her and lowered his head. He stopped when their faces were a breath apart. "Because you'll kiss me first. Then all bets are off.''

"C'MON, BARBARA, you know better."

"You sound like an old man, Dalton," she said into the telephone. "I'm just going to look the place over."

"Where's Landry?"

She frowned. "He's on his way to the cartel office for a meeting with Thomas Shelton. Did you ever check him out? He's the guy who was at the Rose Tattoo the night Breck was shot and he had no reason to be there."

She could hear Dalton shuffling papers before he said, "Yes. Shelton was at the home of a friend. A Mr. Chuck Simms. He owns a garage near Summerville. There was a barbecue. Ten people saw him there until well past midnight."

Her frown deepened. "Thanks." She placed the phone on the cradle and turned to Olivia, who was diligently assembling the newly delivered computer equipment in Cade's living room. "How long until we're up and functional?" Barbara asked as she opened a box that contained her drawing supplies.

"An hour or so."

"I have an errand to run," she said, grabbing her purse. "You can start on the demographic charts as soon as we have desktop publishing."

"I'll have it finished by quitting time," Olivia promised.

"You're a delight," she told the young woman. "Maybe you'll consider relocating to Charleston. I'd be happy to hire you."

Olivia didn't look up from her work, replying, "No thanks, I don't like humid climates."

"I'll be back as soon as possible," Barbara said as she went to the kitchen.

Mrs. Granger was busy preparing a fruit pie, but she stopped working as soon as Barbara walked in. "Yes, miss?"

"I need to use the car."

The housekeeper gave her a puzzled look. Barbara repeated her request, adding, "I won't be gone long."

"Cade didn't leave any instructions about your using a car."

"I saw a fleet of pickup trucks down by the barn. I could use one of those."

Mrs. Granger's brow furrowed. "I'll page Cade and see what he has to say."

Barbara let out a breath. "Don't bother. I'll borrow Olivia's. Thanks so much for your help."

The housekeeper opened her mouth as if to say something, then apparently thought better of it. Good thing, too, Barbara decided. She was getting tired of the woman's aloof treatment.

Unlike Mrs. Granger, Olivia was more than happy to let Barbara take her car. A few minutes later, she was headed down the endless driveway, trying to find a decent radio station.

Barbara stopped at the first gas station she spotted once she was out on the highway. A very accommodating man sold her a soda and a map, and even took the trouble to pencil in the route before wishing her well.

Not only was Olivia the greatest temp in the world, Barbara was also impressed by her neatness. There wasn't a scrap of paper or a piece of lint in the small compact. She was careful not to mess up the immaculate interior. The exterior of the car was another matter. A fine layer of dust was building with each passing mile.

And the miles passed and passed. Oddly, she found the long drive soothing. There was something wonderful about having fresh air blowing through her hair while she sang along with the radio.

She was almost sorry when she spied a large yellow sign in front of a small brick building that read Montana Rentals. After parking next to the only other car in the lot, she tried to calm her unruly hair before stepping into the shop.

She smiled secretly when she was greeted by a pencil-thin young man in a striped uniform shirt. A red bandanna was knotted loosely around his neck and a name badge in the shape of a mailbox was her introduction.

"Hi, Jeff."

"Ma'am," he managed as his Adam's apple bobbed above the knot.

"I'd like to rent a box and I need a money order."

"'Kay." He reached under the desk and brought out two binders. "Small or large box?"

"Large," she said.

He flipped through one of the binders, then passed it across to her. "I need you to fill this out. It'll be thirty bucks for six months or fifty for a whole year."

Barbara did as instructed. "Can I pay for everything at one time?"

"Yes, ma'am." He gulped again and fumbled with the second binder. "How much you need it for?"

When he started to write in the next available space, she said, "Say, Jeff? My car was overheating and making all sorts of noises on my way here. Could you possibly take a look at it?"

The young man appeared flustered.

Batting her eyes coyly enough to make herself gag, Barbara continued her pleading. "I'm new here and I don't know a thing about cars and, well, I'd just hate to get stuck miles away from anything."

"I'm not supposed to leave the shop," he said.

She brightened. "I can stay and listen for the phone. If it rings, I'll run out and get you. Okay? I can fill out this money-order thing while you check under the hood for me."

He shrugged and accepted the key she dangled from one finger. "'Kay, I guess."

Barbara waited until he was outside before she began to thumb through the carbon copies of all the money orders issued in the previous six months. She split her time between looking at the entries and making sure Jeff was busy looking for her nonexistent car woes. Luckily, there weren't that many money orders issued and only a few for sums above five hundred dollars.

Dale Breck had been smart, she conceded when she found the pattern. Laws regulating currency would have prevented him from making large transactions, but he'd found a way around that. Ten days out of each month, a D.B. had purchased five thousand-dollar money orders payable to a Carl Hilton. That had gone on steadily for five months, although the month prior to the murder, the payments had slowed down to only two. Then the day before he came to Charleston, he had purchased a series of money orders in the one day.

Checking to make sure Jeff was still busy, she started to thumb through the mailbox binder and found that Dale Breck was the renter for box 007. Closing the binder, she went over to the wall of mailboxes and found his. She had to get up on tiptoe, but she was able to peer in the tiny glass window. A single letter lay inside.

"I can't find a thing," Jeff said as he returned, wiping his hands on his uniform slacks. "Sorry."

"No problem," Barbara insisted. "I really do appreciate your help."

"Yours is down there," he said, pointing to one of the other boxes.

"Right," Barbara acknowledged, feigning embarrassment. "I've never been very good with numbers."

"You didn't fill out your money order," he said as he scratched his head.

"I, um, changed my mind about that. I'll just pay you for the box." She reached into her wallet and gave him two twenties. He seemed to struggle to make the ten-dollar change.

"This key will get you in the front door anytime. This one is for your box," he explained.

A plan was forming in her head. "I can come in after hours?"

He nodded and gave her a very serious look. "We close off this part of the shop, but the boxes are always open."

"How late are you here?" she asked.

The question very nearly made the kid sweat. "Just till six, ma'am."

"Thank you so much, Jeff. You've been a real help."

He was beaming as she left him. She felt a little guilty for pouring it on so thick, but she was thrilled that her little escapade had yielded so many positive results.

As soon as she pulled out of the parking lot, she took her cell phone from her purse and called the cartel's office. She got the machine. Maybe that was a good sign. Shelton's presentation couldn't have been too good if they were already finished.

Barbara called the ranch and got Mrs. Granger, who provided her with Cade's pager number. She called it and entered her cell-phone number, then left the phone out to await his return call.

Ten minutes passed and still nothing. She called the pager number again and repeated the process as she entered the edge of town. It dawned on her that Jasper had to have a library. Libraries had phone books. Maybe Carl Hilton was listed.

She was feeling quite proud of herself as she turned up and down the quaint streets until she found a small public library next to the sheriff's office. She sneered in its general direction, not overly fond of Sheriff Seth Landry based on their one meeting.

Putting her phone in her purse with the ringer volume turned up to high, she parked and went into the library. Aside from a librarian who looked older than some of literature's great works, she had the place to herself. She asked about the reference section and was sent to the far wall, where she found what she was looking for.

Moistening her finger, she began flipping through the residential listings for Jasper. No Carl Hilton. She was about to check the business listings when her phone chirped and echoed through the still room. Ignoring the silent, reproachful stare of the librarian, she grabbed it and excitedly began to talk.

"You won't believe what I—"

Barbara fell silent as soon as the sound on the other end registered. She heard a rich, deep man's voice, but it wasn't Cade. It was Elvis, singing "Don't."

Chapter Ten

Cade walked into Seth's office without knocking. He found Barbara seated on the worn leather sofa, her hands tightly wrapped around a mug of coffee.

Her expression was drawn as she looked up at him with frightened, guarded eyes. A bolt of rage surged through him.

"How long ago did he call?"

"A half hour," she replied.

Her voice held the quiet strength he had grown to admire. Placing one hand on her leg, he turned to Seth. "Thanks for your help."

His cousin shrugged. "I'm just glad I was in the office. That detective in Charleston is working on getting the records from her cell-phone company. I sent one of my guys out to your spread for Barbara's temp. He'll bring her back to town to pick up her car."

"That wasn't necessary," Cade heard Barbara say.

"I didn't think Cade would want you driving," Seth explained.

Barbara's demeanor changed then. "Sheriff, in

case you haven't noticed, I'm fully capable of making my own decisions.''

"Like traipsing around the back roads of Montana?'' Cade challenged.

"I think I'll let you two talk,'' Seth mumbled before slipping from the room.

"Well?'' Cade persisted.

She shrugged away from him. "Don't take that tone with me,'' she warned. "I had an idea, so I went to check it out.''

Cade battled a strong urge to throttle the woman. "You're supposed to stay at the ranch. I promised Dalton I'd watch after you.''

Rolling her eyes at him, she stood and abandoned the coffee cup. "I don't require a sitter, Landry.''

"You do if you're going to take unnecessary chances.''

She regarded him with an air of superiority that made his blood boil. "I just went to Montana Rentals,'' she said.

"And put yourself in a position for Elvis to contact you.''

"My phone would've rung no matter where I was,'' she argued. "I only got spooked because I was expecting you, not some veiled threat from that lunatic.''

"Me?''

She gaped at him. "I paged you, Cade. Twice.''

He uttered a quick oath. "I must've left my pager

at the office.'' Her ''your-fault-not-mine'' look didn't improve his temper.

''Have you ever heard of a man named Carl Hilton?'' she asked.

The name didn't ring any bells and he told her as much. ''Why?''

Barbara explained about the money orders and the letter waiting for Dale in his box. ''There's no Carl Hilton in the phone book. He must have an unlisted number.''

''Seth can check.''

''Maybe the letter waiting for Dale is from Hilton.'' Barbara grabbed up her purse. ''It's after six, so it should be safe for us to go back and—''

''Hold up,'' he said, raising one hand. ''You aren't Nancy Drew.''

She sneered at him. ''And you aren't the one Elvis wants dead.''

''Barbara.'' He said her name in as reasonable a tone as he could muster. ''Tomorrow Seth and Dalton can work out whatever they need to get that letter. Besides, you don't even know if it's relevant to the murder.''

She crossed her arms in front of her. ''But it *might* be,'' she scoffed, ''which means it *might* be the key to solving the murder, which means I *won't* get any more calls or visits from Elvis.''

''I forbid it.''

''I don't really care what you forbid,'' she said. ''I'm not going to sit around waiting for Elvis to make another move. For all I know, he made that call from around the corner. I want this to end. Now.''

''It will,'' he reasoned. ''We just have to be patient and—''

''You be patient. I'm going back to Montana Rentals.''

''Are you walking?'' he taunted.

She glared at him. ''No. I'm going to call Helena and rent a car.''

''Over my dead body.''

''Don't get my hopes up,'' she replied. ''You aren't going to stop me, Landry.''

''I can tell Seth what you're planning. I'm sure breaking into a post-office box is some sort of crime.''

''Fine. He can arrest me after I've taken a look.''

''You're not being rational, Barbara.''

''I'm being proactive.'' She picked up the telephone from Seth's desk and pushed three buttons, then asked for a listing for a car-rental agency.

Cade stepped over and disconnected the call. The set of her jaw and the fierce light in her eyes told him no amount of argument or reason would stop her. Against his better instincts, he heard himself agreeing to act as her chauffeur.

''It's no wonder you almost got yourself killed,'' he grumbled a short while later when he was parked in front of Montana Rentals.

''Didn't you ever learn that if you don't have

something nice to say, you shouldn't say anything at all?''

"Ever hear that stupid is as stupid does?'' he countered as he followed her into the deserted building.

He watched as Barbara went directly to a mailbox on the upper tier and looked in. "It's gone.''

"What?'' Cade moved behind her. "Are you sure you saw something in there earlier?''

"Definitely,'' she replied forcefully. "So who took it?''

"Got me,'' Cade said. "Can we go back to the ranch now?''

She shook her head. The action caused a few strands of her hair to tickle his face. The air between them filled with the scent of her shampoo. Less than an arm's length separated them. He looked down and started thinking about things other than some wayward letter. He wondered if his attraction was turning into some sort of obsession. He'd been seconds away from watching her commit a federal offense and all he could remember was what it had been like to hold her against him. But it was more than that.

Learning that Elvis had called her had made him angry, but it had done something else, too. His first thought had been for her. For her safety. The knowledge that the killer could reach her so easily a second time had caught him off guard.

Now, as he looked down at her, he knew he was interested in more than catching Elvis. He'd been attracted to Barbara ever since their first meeting. She

was a beautiful woman. But it was more than her
beauty that had him tied in knots at present. It was
acknowledging that his feelings went deeper than
mere desire. Grudgingly, he realized he admired her
strength even if he did find her infuriating at times.
Whom was he kidding? He didn't just want her or
admire her. The threat from Elvis had cinched it. He
was on the verge of falling in love with her.

Great going, Cade! he silently admonished himself.
*You weren't supposed to fall in love with her. You
were supposed to lie to her.*

"NICE PLACE," BARBARA commented after surveying
Dale Breck's single-story home. Empty flower boxes
framed the windows above long-neglected beds.

Cade retrieved a key from a rock next to the front
walkway and they went inside. They were greeted by
darkness and a musty smell. When he turned on the
lights, she noted that Dale hadn't been much of a
housekeeper. The place wasn't dirty, just cluttered.
Newspapers were piled in various places and she
guessed it had been quite some time since anyone had
dusted the slightly dated furniture.

The early-American decor was accented by a collection of photographs in tarnished silver frames. She
reached for one, blew off a cobweb from one corner
and studied the woman's face. Barbara guessed she'd
been in her late forties at the time the picture was
taken. Judging from the clothing, she also thought the
picture was at least fifteen years old.

"That's Mary, Dale's wife," Cade explained.

"She was pretty," Barbara absently remarked as she placed the photograph back among the others. It struck her that there were so many pictures that the top of the table looked a little like a shrine. "He must have loved her."

Cade's only response was a slight nod. "What are we looking for?" he asked. "Dalton already had the state police search the house. They didn't find anything."

Barbara shrugged and began thumbing through a stack of magazines on the coffee table. "Anything that might explain who Carl Hilton is."

"Did you ever consider that Dale might have been Carl Hilton? Maybe it was all a front so he could keep the cash for himself."

Barbara dismissed his theory outright. "He went to much too much trouble to siphon off funds just to line his own pockets. My guess is that Carl Hilton was blackmailing Dale." Cade had planted himself in the center of the room. She felt his eyes follow her as she went from pile to pile, checking item after item. "You could help," she suggested as his constant watching began to wear thin on her nerves.

"Sure, I'll see if Dale died with any beer in the fridge."

She cast him a disdainful look before returning to her search. It shouldn't have mattered that Cade was treating her suspicions like folly. But it did. Knowing that was almost as annoying as working under his watchful gaze.

She heard him moving around in the adjoining room and her mind produced a vivid image of him. It was like he was indelibly imprinted on her brain. She knew there was a slight swagger in his walk. That his eyes flashed hot and cold depending on his mood. He was a very mercurial man and that wasn't her preference. Still, she seemed drawn to him regardless of that fact. Cade Landry personified everything she didn't want in a man. To keep from remembering how wonderful it had felt to be kissed by him, she started a mental list of all the reasons she should keep her distance. For one thing, his cockiness bordered on arrogance.

A little voice in her mind countered, *He's as sure of himself as you are of yourself.*

He apparently saw nothing wrong with punching someone as a means of resolving a conflict.

He was just a father protecting his daughter. Didn't you get physical with the doctor who killed Claire?

Cade always thinks he knows what's best.

So do you. You are unyielding when you make a decision.

Cade doesn't take no for an answer.

Aren't you glad he didn't?

"Getting anywhere?" Cade asked when he returned with two bottles of beer.

Averting her eyes, she said, "Not really."

"There's nothing in the kitchen."

Accepting the beer, Barbara followed a narrow hallway and opened the first door. It was a small bedroom, but it had no bed. Instead, boxes were stacked neatly against one wall. She stepped forward and read the notation on the side of the top box. "Western Little Theater?"

"It's a dinner theater in Helena," Cade explained.

"Was Dale an actor?"

"Seems he was," Cade replied wryly. The sadness in his voice tugged at her heart.

With his help, she pulled down the top box and lifted the lid. Inside she found some yellowed scripts, some playbills and an assortment of black-and-white production photographs.

"Isn't that Mary?" she asked, pointing to a woman in a group shot dressed as Eliza Doolittle.

"Yeah." He took the picture from her and looked on the back. "This was taken more than twenty years ago."

Barbara and Cade spent more than two hours going through the remaining boxes. The contents were pretty much the same in all of them. Apparently, Mary Breck had saved everything associated with more than three decades of doing amateur theater. Barbara might have thought it odd that Dale had kept it all for more than ten years after her death, but then she remembered the photo gallery in the living room.

"Want another beer?"

Barbara didn't look up from the box to say,

"Please." Her throat was dry from all the dust in the air. The last collection of photographs was dated the month Dale's wife died. Barbara studied each picture in turn. Mary looked healthy and happy dressed in Shakespearean garb. "I guess she didn't die as a result of a prolonged illness," she mused as she surveyed another cast photo.

The black-and-white shot contained more than thirty people. Because of the heavy makeup and costuming, Barbara had to pull out the playbill in order to pick Mary from among the ensemble.

"Cade!" she called as she scrambled to her feet. "Cade!"

She met him in the hallway, nearly slamming into him as she waved the photograph and the playbill in the air like some out-of-control cheerleader.

"Yes?"

She beamed up at him. "I found Carl Hilton."

It took two more hours—and Cade's help—for Barbara to organize the years of memorabilia. She felt positively giddy as she reconstructed ten years of Mary's life in the theater prior to her death. And Carl Hilton had played a role all along.

"I'm impressed," Cade said.

"Thank you."

"Let's take this stuff back home," he suggested. "I'm sure Dalton will be interested in it."

Barbara carefully gathered up the items. "Dalton is welcome to it after we've had a chance to go to some of these theaters to see if Carl Hilton is still acting.''

''Isn't it enough that you found him?'' Cade asked as they stepped into the brisk night. ''Let the police find a connection between Hilton and Dale's murder. Assuming there is one.''

''Don't rain on my parade, Landry,'' she warned. ''I'll tell Dalton all about this, but I'm here and he isn't.''

''You're here to stay alive,'' Cade said. ''Not chase after some actor Dale's long-dead wife knew.''

''The same actor Dale was paying thousands of dollars in blackmail to every month,'' Barbara reminded him. ''How can this *not* be the key to why he was killed?''

Cade played devil's advocate all the way back to the Lazy L. Barbara refused to allow her enthusiasm to diminish.

Soon Elvis would be nothing but a memory. Everything seemed brighter to her now that she had something solid. She loved the way the stars twinkled in the massive Montana sky. Right then, she even loved the chilly air.

''What a beautiful night,'' she said as she lingered on the porch.

''Technically,'' Cade said as he leaned against the railing, ''it's morning.''

Moonlight cast shadows across his handsome face. ''Then it's a beautiful morning,'' she corrected. She spun on the balls of her feet. "For the first time in days, I feel like there's an end to this ordeal."

"I'm sorry being here has been an ordeal."

She stopped and moved next to him. "It's been different."

"Is that good or bad?"

Pensively, she twisted her hair around one finger. "Both. Being around you is…complicated."

She heard him take a deep breath. "It isn't over yet."

Turning sideways, she made contact with his solid form. Need, real and palpable, erupted inside her. "Sorry," she mumbled as she took a step back.

It felt to Barbara as if they were the only two people on earth. Cade reached out and caught a lock of her hair. Quietly, he studied it with those intense eyes of his. "You're very beautiful when you're happy."

"Thank you."

Her response seemed to surprise him.

"What?" she prompted.

Slowly, he smiled. "I was expecting you to bite my head off for mentioning it."

A grin tugged at the corners of her mouth. "Poor Cade. Having a hard time dealing with a woman who doesn't throw herself at you?"

"As a matter of fact," he began as his hand moved to her face, "yes. But only because I want you more than I want my next breath."

Her chest constricted at his words. Forcing lightness into her voice, she said, "We don't always get everything we want."

His gaze held her. "Toss me a crumb here, Barbara. It wasn't easy for me to admit that to you."

So much for lightness. Especially when his thumb began a maddening series of circles against her cheek. Her lips parted but no words came out. She had none to offer. Surely he felt the race of her pulse, could see the uneven tempo of her breathing because he was touching her.

The intelligent thing to do was simply to walk away. But when Cade ran the pad of his thumb over her lower lip, it melted everything inside her. He was alternately rough and gentle, slow and urgent.

She was amazed that the pressure of his thumb could be so erotic. As he increased the friction, he inspired anticipation. She wanted more than his touch. She needed to feel his mouth on hers. "Kiss me."

His eyes flashed as he bent forward, barely making contact. She experienced the first few seconds of the kiss through a mist of ferocious need. It wasn't enough. Winding her arms around him, she drew herself against his taut body.

Her hands raced up into his hair, grasping him and pressing their mouths closer together. Cade's response was guarded and controlled. No matter what she tried, she couldn't seem to unleash the passion they'd shared in his study.

Conceding defeat, she broke off the kiss and rested

her hands against his chest. "Sorry. I guess I misread the situation."

Cade held her fast. "Look at me."

She lifted her eyes to his. They were dark, smoldering and sexy. His breath spilled over her face in warm, ragged waves. She opened her mouth to speak.

"Tell me what you want," he instructed.

She felt her face flame. "I would think that was obvious."

"You want me to kiss you?"

She nodded mutely.

"Is that all you want? Because once we start, I'll want a hell of a lot more than just a kiss."

A shiver worked its way along her spine. Anticipation and need were living, growing things inside her as she considered his words. There would be no turning back. Their relationship would be forever changed if she surrendered to her own strong want. Her fingers wrapped around taut muscle. She could feel the heat of his body. Sense his desire was as fervent as her own. Slowly, she peered up into his intense gaze....

Chapter Eleven

"Good morning," Mrs. Granger said when Barbara appeared in the kitchen close to noon.

Olivia was seated at the table having a glass of juice. She started to get up, but Barbara told her to stay. "I'm sorry I slept so late."

"No problem," Olivia answered easily. "I've finished the charts and I went ahead and set up a template for the storyboards in the animation program."

Barbara was impressed. "Where's Cade?" she asked the housekeeper.

"Went out early this morning," she replied. "Said to let you know he'd be back in the early afternoon."

It shouldn't have come as any great shock that the man was avoiding her. First she had thrown herself at him on the porch, then she had just left him there. Surely she wasn't on his list of favorite people right now.

"Thank you," she told Mrs. Granger. "I've been meaning to tell you how much I've enjoyed your meals. You're a good cook."

"A simple cook," the housekeeper acknowledged without any real trace of pride. "I like simple things."

Realizing flattery was a wasted effort on the stalwart woman, she and Olivia headed into the living room and began work. Barbara did some rough sketches for a thirty-second spot from memory.

"You're talented," Olivia remarked.

Barbara smiled. "When I was young, I wanted to sit on some cliff in New England painting seascapes."

"Why didn't you?"

Barbara chuckled. "My father convinced me that painting wasn't a very practical thing to do. It was fine as a hobby, according to him. And sure to attract great husband prospects. When I heard that, I stopped painting."

Olivia was punching holes in the demographic charts and placing them in color-coordinated binders. "You never wanted to get married?"

"Never is a long time," Barbara mused. "I guess I've been waiting for Mr. Right, not Mr. Right Now." *Which one is Cade?*

"But you have money," Olivia argued.

Glancing up at the young woman, Barbara regarded her for a moment. "Money has nothing to do with relationships, Olivia."

"The lack of it sure does."

She smiled. "You don't think you can be poor and happy, huh?"

Olivia's dark eyes flashed. "I think it's unfair that

some people get everything handed to them while the rest of us have to work hard just to survive.''

"Pretty cynical."

Olivia shrugged apologetically. "I'm finished here. I thought I'd drive into Helena this afternoon to have the charts enlarged at the printer's. If that's okay with you?''

"Great," Barbara said. "Treat yourself to a decadent lunch while you're out." She went to her purse and pulled out some money to hand over. "Think of it as my way of apologizing for last night. I hope I didn't inconvenience you too much."

"It was no problem," Olivia insisted as she put the bills in the pocket of her dress. "Is there anything else I can do for you?''

Barbara shook her head. "No. But don't bother coming back this afternoon."

Olivia looked stricken. "I can go to the print shop on my own time if—''

"I'll pay you for the day," Barbara assured her. "I have to finish these drawings before you can scan them into the computer. There's really no point in having you sit here and watch me do it. Goof off for the rest of the day. We'll get back to work tomorrow morning.''

"Thank you, Miss Prather."

"Barbara," she corrected easily.

"Barbara," Olivia repeated. "Oh, did Mrs. Granger tell you about the phone call?''

"What phone call?''

Olivia put the charts in her briefcase. "It was someone named Ross."

"Okay," Barbara said, hoping to reassure her timid assistant. Olivia was a great worker, but she seemed so tense. It was almost as if she expected Barbara to grow fangs and attack. She chalked it up to youth and inexperience. As competent as Olivia was, Barbara had no doubt she would learn to hold her own someday.

She finished the last sketch for the shorter commercial and set it aside. It was nearly one, which meant Cade would be back soon. Barbara knew she shouldn't care, but she did. The house seemed lonely and empty without Cade in it. If she were being honest, she would admit that she was lonely and empty, too.

She wasn't ready to be honest.

Using the phone next to the computer, Barbara dialed Dalton's number. He wasn't in, but she left word with the duty sergeant to let him know she had returned his call.

She heard the back door open and close, then the unmistakable sound of Cade's footsteps. Sheer will permitted her to wait a full minute before she pretended to casually stroll to the kitchen.

He greeted her with an easy smile. "Mrs. Granger tells me you've been hard at work."

"Mrs. Granger didn't tell me that Dalton called," Barbara said.

Cade finished a long drink of water before replying, "I talked to him."

"And?" she pressed.

"Nothing concrete yet. I've got to catch a shower."

Concrete? "What does that mean?" she asked as she followed him from the kitchen.

"It means the phone company's computer system is still trying to locate the origin of the call."

Barbara nodded and stopped short of following him up the stairs. "I was thinking of going to some of those theaters this afternoon."

"Think again," he called over his shoulder.

"I don't need your permission!"

He ignored her.

"C'mon, Cade. What can it hurt?"

He stopped at the second-floor landing and looked down at her. "You can get yourself killed, for one."

"You're being overly dramatic. All I'm going to do is ask around. Don't be so negative."

"I'm tired, Barbara. For some reason, I didn't sleep very well last night. Any guesses why?"

Ouch, she thought as she wandered out to the porch. Rolling her head around, she eased some of the stiffness in her neck. Without any real direction in mind, she found herself walking down to where some horses were grazing near the barn. The brilliant afternoon sun warmed the chill in the air.

"Want to ride?"

She recognized T.J. and smiled at him.

"Once was enough, thanks. How's your jaw?"

He blushed. "Not as bad as it could have been. Cade pulled his punch."

"If that was pulled, I'd hate to see a real one."

"Yes, ma'am," T.J. agreed. "Course, I've never known Cade to hit a man that didn't need hitting."

She shrugged. "Nice to know he has standards."

"What?"

"Nothing," she assured him. "How far is Helena from here?"

"About two hours." Then, slightly embarrassed, he went on to add, "More if you do the speed limit."

"Is there anyplace I can rent a car around here?"

He shook his head. "There's a dealership west of Jasper that rents sometimes, but Hank only gives cars out to folks he knows. Why don't you just use the Bronco?" he suggested. "Slick always leaves the keys in the ignition."

"Really?" Barbara managed to inquire without yelping with delight. "Where is this Bronco?"

T.J. hooked his thumb over his shoulder. "Other side of the barn."

After sneaking into the house for her purse, Barbara stopped long enough to jot Cade a quick note. To keep her conscience clear, she taped it to the screen of her computer, where he would find it—eventually.

Climbing into the vehicle, she tossed her purse on the passenger seat and started the engine. It roared to life, then died just as quickly. Murdered by Cade's hand.

"What do you think you're doing?" he demanded.

His hair was still wet from the shower and his shirt was open. The breeze lifted the edges, revealing tanned skin and taut, rippling muscles. Seeing his bared torso didn't exactly help her focus on the matter at hand.

"I wasn't stealing it, Landry. I left you a note."

"Get out." Yanking the door open, he gave her a look that wordlessly dared her not to comply.

Lifting her arms in surrender, she matched his stubborn expression with one of her own. "Fine. I'll just have to be more patient and wait until I can have a rental delivered."

"What part of all this don't you understand?" Cade lectured as they walked back toward the house. "You aren't going anywhere to look for Carl Hilton."

"Am, too."

A sound rumbled in his throat. "My daughter has more sense than you do."

"Maybe that's because *she* has a car," Barbara retorted.

"Seth has already looked for Carl Hilton. He doesn't have a current Montana driver's license. Now will you get off this kick?"

"No," she answered him. "Maybe Carl Hilton doesn't drive."

"Everyone in Montana drives."

"Everyone but me," she groused when he held the kitchen door for her. "You can't prevent me from renting a car, Landry."

Their eyes locked in a silent battle. He blinked first. "I should lock you in your room."

She smiled up at him. "But you won't because you want to find Elvis just as much as I do."

"I used to think so," he muttered. "Come with me."

She followed him to his study and stood by while he called Thomas Shelton to reschedule a meeting.

"You met with him yesterday," she commented, hoping to get a feel for how things were going for her competition.

"We got interrupted when his office called him," Cade explained.

Her eyes were drawn to his chest as he fastened the buttons of his shirt. He stuffed the shirt into the waistband of his jeans, then used a length of rawhide to tie his still-damp hair back. He probably didn't realize that in doing so, he flexed inspiring biceps. He didn't—but she sure did.

Barbara bit the inside of her mouth to force her brain to think of anything other than his impressive body. The same body he had so willingly placed at her disposal. Even the pinch of her own teeth couldn't rid her of the memory of being in his arms. Mentally, she berated herself for having so little self-control where he was concerned.

"What's wrong now?" Cade asked, slightly testy.

She shook her head. "What could be wrong?" *Just because I have a major case of lust going on for a client doesn't mean anything is wrong.*

"DALE'S FUNERAL WILL BE tomorrow afternoon," he told her an hour later when they were on the road to Helena.

"Is there anything I can do to help?"

"Come with me," he said without hesitation.

"Sure," she said. "I'll need to get something to wear while we're out."

"No problem," he said. "I thought I'd drop in on Jess for a little while so you can shop. By then, most of the theaters will be open."

"I hadn't thought of that," Barbara admitted.

He gave her a sidelong look. "Good thing you have me around then, huh?"

"Something like that," she relented. "How come you aren't married, Landry?"

"I was."

"Did you like it?"

"You don't usually get a divorce if you like it."

"Sorry," Barbara mumbled. "I guess happy marriages are few and far between, huh?"

"I'll bet all your friends are single. Most are divorced, right?"

"Wrong," she said on a little laugh. "All my friends are married except for Susan."

"Susan? The New Age waitress at the Rose Tattoo?"

Barbara chuckled. "I see she made an impression."

"She's…unique. So how come you're not married?"

"How come everyone keeps asking me that?"

"It must be your hearth-and-home personality," he teased.

She sat straighter in her seat. "I like my work, Landry. Is that a crime?"

He shook his head. "Not to me. A woman with her own identity and direction in life is very, very sexy."

"Did you read that on the cover of *Cosmo?*"

"I happen to believe it," he defended. "I hope my daughter takes the time to find out who she is before she gets involved."

Barbara regarded him for a long moment. "I'm sure she will."

She watched as a frown curved his lips downward. "I don't know. She's had boys on the brain for the past eighteen months. I think it's getting worse."

"It's her job to have boys on the brain," Barbara assured him. "We females have all those frogs to kiss before we find a prince. It's the law."

"I think I've just been called a frog," he joked.

"I was speaking generally, not specifically."

"You're doing a real job on my ego, Barbara."

"Landry," she warned, "don't start that again. In case you hadn't noticed, we were having a real conversation. Don't ruin it by beating a dead horse."

"Back to real conversation," he agreed, putting her at ease. "I think you began this gabfest by asking me why I'm not married. I hated women on principle when I first got divorced. Not being able to see your child every day will do that to a man."

"How old was Jessica when you got divorced?"

"Almost three. She and Whitney moved to Helena with her folks."

"When did your wife die?" Barbara asked.

"Four years ago. Jess took it hard, but I think moving back to the ranch helped."

"Then why is she going to school in Helena?"

Cade shrugged. "She can get a better education there and it helps my former in-laws cope with their loss."

"You're a nice man, Landry."

He looked slightly flustered for a minute, then joked, "So how come you won't sleep with me?"

"Conversation interruptus," she teased right back.

"I'll take you to a small shop in town. You'll love it."

"How do you know?"

He winked and said, "I packed for you, remember?"

CADE PICKED HER UP an hour later as arranged. "It takes all this to dress for a funeral?" he queried as he eyed the garment bags and shoe boxes she laid on the back seat.

"This is one of the advantages of having money," she assured him. "I can indulge myself."

"Are you hungry?"

She shook her head. "Not really. I'd prefer to go Carl-searching."

"You can be single-minded."

"It's one of my charms."

Cade had a whole list of her charms, but her stubbornness wasn't on it. Her eyes were at the top. He would have gladly spent the evening looking into them, watching the way they caught the light. His brain was muddled. It had been ever since she'd left him standing in the dark. He didn't want to feel this way. He couldn't afford to fall in love with her.

He couldn't stop himself.

"Hello?" Barbara's voice called to him.

"Sorry. The Western Little Theater is just ahead."

Cade parked in the lot and led Barbara up to the ticket window. A young girl stopped smacking a wad of chewing gum long enough to ask, "Can I help you?"

"We're looking for an actor," Barbara explained. "Carl Hilton?"

The girl shook her head. "No one in the show by that name."

"He may have retired," Cade said. "Is the manager around?"

The girl hopped off her stool and disappeared into the building. When she returned, she had a costumed, middle-aged man in Pan-Cake makeup in tow.

"Yes?" he asked.

"We're looking for Carl Hilton," Cade repeated. "He used to be active at this theater."

The gentleman nodded. "I knew Carl."

"Knew?" Barbara asked.

The man smiled gently. "Yes, ma'am. Carl passed away."

"When?" Cade pressed.

The man seemed taken aback. "Ten years almost. Fall, 1991."

"Thank you," Cade said as he placed his hand on Barbara's back. "Sorry to have bothered you before the show."

Cade mulled over the information as he guided Barbara back to the car and slid behind the wheel.

"No pun intended, but that was a dead end."

"Hardly," Barbara fairly gushed. "Carl Hilton died at about the same time as Mary Breck. Doesn't that seem strange to you?"

He shrugged. "Dale's wife died of heart failure, so, no."

"Are you sure about the cause of death?"

"Positive. Want to stop for dinner? I don't have to be back at the Lazy L until ten," he said.

"Curfew?" she teased.

"Actually, Thomas Shelton is coming by."

Barbara ate without much enthusiasm and he didn't blame her. Carl Hilton had seemed like a strong lead.

"Why was Dale buying money orders for a dead man?" he wondered aloud.

"My thought exactly," Barbara said as they left the small coffee shop. "Unless Dale knew Carl was dead and was using his identity to hide his theft."

Cade felt the sting of his friend's betrayal again. Raking one hand through his hair, he tried to think of an explanation that made sense. "If it was just about cash flow, I think Dale would've come to me."

"Which means I was right. He was paying blackmail, not stealing for himself," Barbara agreed. "What could he have done?"

Cade thought long and hard. "I've known him most of my life. I can't imagine anything that would've led to blackmail."

"And murder," Barbara reminded him just as they reached the house. "Speaking of murder, I see Shelton is here to kill my chances at landing the account."

Cade shook his head and chuckled. "Dale promised him a shot at the account, Barbara. I can't blow him off."

"I know," she said grudgingly. "Help me get all this stuff inside. If you promise not to show Shelton any of my work, I promise not to listen at the door while he explains how badly his ideas will pale in comparison with mine."

"You have an evil streak," Cade whispered.

Barbara walked ahead of him, her arms filled with boxes. He followed, carting the heavy garment bag. He was two steps below her when he saw the red beam of a rifle's laser scope fix on the back of her head.

Chapter Twelve

Everything happened in a split second. Barbara heard the crack of a gunshot. Then a crushing weight slammed into her. The next moment, all the air rushed from her body as she hit the steps.

I can't breathe, she thought in a panic. *Was I shot?*

In the eerie silence that followed, Barbara realized she felt no pain.

"Are you all right?" Cade asked.

When he rolled off her, she sucked in deep gulps of air. Cade took hold of her shoulders and seemed to be looking for the injury. Giving her a gentle shake, he repeated the question.

Looking up into his eyes, she read his fear. Barbara shook her head. "I'm okay."

His relief was palpable as he pulled her into his arms. "Thank God," he whispered.

"I need some help here," she heard Shelton say in a trembling voice.

In unison, she and Cade looked over and saw him

propped against the side of the house. His shirtsleeve was bright red and he was clutching his shoulder.

Reflexively, Barbara started to stand, but Cade yanked her down behind the shield of his large body. He stayed in front of her as they crawled closer to Shelton. The man's taut face was white, his expression a blend of shock and pain.

Cade kept himself between Barbara and the direction the shot had come from. After managing to open the front door, he shoved her inside, then grabbed Shelton by the shirt and dragged him to safety, as well.

Mrs. Granger appeared in the foyer, toting a shotgun.

"Stay down!" she heard Cade call.

As if it were an everyday occurrence, the housekeeper slipped to her knees and went to assist Cade at Shelton's side.

"Call 911," Cade instructed as he yanked his shirt over his head, wadded it into a ball and pressed it against Shelton's wound. "Hold this," he told the housekeeper.

Shelton winced and made a strangled sound. Barbara was frozen in place as she watched Cade and his housekeeper at work.

"Move, Barbara!" Cade yelled. "We need an ambulance."

Shakily, she slid along the wood floor, then crawled into the living room. Blindly, she felt along the desk until she found the phone, then yanked it into her lap.

Blood pounded in her ears and her hands were trembling, making it almost impossible to complete the call.

"This is 911. What is your emergency?" a female voice asked dispassionately.

"There's someone shooting at us. Um, we need an ambulance."

"You're calling from the Lazy L, right?"

"Yes," Barbara hissed. "We need help! He's still out there!"

"Are you hurt?" the operator asked evenly.

Some part of her brain knew it was the woman's job to calmly collect details, but Barbara was feeling anything but calm. "It isn't me! Please?" she pleaded in a frenzy. "He's bleeding and—"

"I've already alerted the sheriff and the paramedics," the woman promised. "I need you to take some deep breaths now. It's important for you to remain calm."

"Cade!" Barbara called when she watched him grab the shotgun and start for the door. "What are you doing? You can't go out there!"

Her protests fell on deaf ears. Frantically, Barbara watched as Cade weaved and bobbed his way across the front lawn, heading for a thicket of trees.

"He's going to get himself killed!" she cried.

Minutes passed like hours. Barbara listened and watched. Her heart was racing. *Please don't let anything happen to him!*

The sound of approaching sirens brought her some

measure of relief. At least Cade wouldn't be out there alone with the lunatic.

Ignoring Mrs. Granger's cautionary words, Barbara went out the door and bounded down the steps to meet the sheriff's car. An ambulance came to a screeching halt behind the car. An unbroken line of police vehicles followed. Officers with guns drawn soon ringed the front lawn.

Over the wail of sirens and crackling radios, Barbara yelled that Cade had gone after the shooter. A deputy had her arm and was dragging her, struggling, back up onto the porch. "He's out there!" Barbara yelled, pointing toward the trees. "You have to help him!"

"We will," the deputy assured her as he walked her up the steps. "You need to get inside, ma'am."

Reluctantly, Barbara stepped over the shoes and clothing scattered all over the floor. Turning sideways, she went past the gurney where Shelton was receiving treatment. The deputy wouldn't let her near a window. She had no idea what was happening. No idea if Cade was safe.

A chill rippled along her spine. Her mind conjured up all sorts of images. None of them good.

The deputy reached into the breast pocket of his uniform and retrieved a small pad and a pen. "What happened?"

At first she ignored him, but he was persistent. "All I know is that one minute I was walking, then the next minute Cade was on top of me and Shelton had been shot. I didn't see anything.''

As he made a note of her remarks, Barbara heard another vehicle, then dogs whining and barking.

"That's the K-9 unit," the deputy said. "If the shooter is out there, we'll find him."

Somehow that wasn't comforting. Cade had been gone for what seemed like hours. She wanted to know where he was. She wanted to know that Cade was unhurt.

Pacing in the study under the watchful eye of the deputy, Barbara tried not to let panic get the better of her. "Where is he?" she whispered. "Why hasn't he come back?"

Another officer appeared at the door. "EMS is going to take Mr. Shelton to the hospital."

"Is it serious?" she asked.

"It's a clean through and through," the officer said. "He won't need anything more than some stitches."

"Good," Barbara sighed, feeling guilty that she hadn't shown proper concern. "May I talk to him first?"

The two deputies conferred silently, then she was allowed to return to the foyer. Shelton was half-sitting on the stretcher, his shoulder bandaged.

"I'm so sorry," Barbara said.

Shelton stared at her with cold, hard eyes. "A lot of good that does me."

He was wheeled out as she repeated her apology.

Barbara watched as he was loaded into the waiting ambulance. Brushing her hair away from her face, she felt the deputy grasp her arm.

Catching sight of two silhouettes on the lawn, she yanked free and dashed outside. Running full out, she reached Cade in seconds. Without thinking, she leaped into his arms and hugged him fiercely.

He held her off the ground with one arm. She could feel the rapid beat of his heart. Feel the tension in his large body. Releasing him, she slipped to the ground and swung at him. Her open hand connected with his bare, solid chest. "What kind of idiot are you?" she demanded.

He seemed genuinely shocked as he handed the shotgun to Seth. "The kind of idiot who got the plate number of the car as he was driving away."

"You could've been killed!" she fumed.

He grinned down at her. "But I wasn't."

"Don't placate me, Landry," she warned. "It was incredibly stupid of you to go tearing after that lunatic."

He shrugged his shoulders. "Seemed like a good idea at the time."

Seth cleared his throat. "I need to get your statement, Cade. Can the two of you battle this out later?"

"WE NEED TO TALK," Cade said when he burst into her bedroom a few hours later.

All the time and effort he'd spent preparing his little speech to explain why he'd deceived her flew out the window when he caught his first glimpse of her. She was standing by the window, wearing a pale silk nightgown. She looked almost ethereal in the moonlight. The silk was like a second skin, covering and revealing all at once. Her face was a vision, framed by her mane of red hair.

"I was hoping you'd come," she said softly.

"Barbara?" he whispered, nearly strangling on the lump in his throat. "I need—"

She closed the distance between them. He could smell her perfume as she reached up and placed her delicate fingertips over his mouth. "I don't want to talk, Cade."

"This is—"

"What I want," Barbara finished for him. "Just for a few hours, I'd like to forget about everything."

"But—"

"Hush," she murmured as she placed a kiss on his chin.

The sensation of her body against his was his undoing. Shutting his eyes, he swallowed the groan that rumbled through him. "Barbara," he managed between clenched teeth, "we need to talk before this goes any further."

Taking one of his hands, she brought it up and placed it against her breast. "We'll talk later," she promised. "Please, Cade?"

His mouth locked with hers. It was a long, deep, meaningful kiss that curled her toes. She heard the scrape of his boots as he lifted her, then felt herself being carried into the adjoining room. She was set down gently next to a huge bed. His bed.

Reaching up, she lightly ran the tip of her fingernail over his lower lip. She could feel the outline of his powerfully built thighs where they rubbed hers.

His expression stilled and grew serious when Barbara pressed herself against him. Cade placed his hands at her waist. For an instant, she thought he might push her away.

"We really do need to get a few things straight."

She shook her head and grew bolder as she held him against her. "Later."

His hesitation lasted less than a second before his lips found hers. Tentative and testing, his mouth settled over hers. She responded by allowing her lips to part, urging his sweet exploration. He groaned as his arms encircled her, pulling her so close that Barbara could feel every solid inch of him.

Her mind reeled from the blatant sensuality of his kiss. It was as if a flash fire had ignited and it was quickly burning out of control. Her hands moved down from his face until she could feel his heart beat furiously. He gripped her more tightly, causing her back to arch. Cade moaned against her mouth.

Emotions and sensations melted together and coursed through her veins. Her entire body tingled with life and she began to work on the buttons of his shirt. Guided by the powerful force of her desire, Barbara unbuttoned his shirt, pushed aside the fabric and ran her palms over his heated flesh. His breath fell hotly over her skin when he raised his head. She was about to utter a protest when he lifted her up and placed her on the bed.

His lips were on her throat, tasting the faintly floral scent of her skin. She felt so delicate and yet the strength of her passion had completely obliterated his need to tell her everything. He didn't want to think about it now. If he did, he knew he'd have to stop.

He lay beside her, his one leg wedged between hers. Placing his hand at her waist, Cade kissed the tip of her nose before renewing his interest in her throat. He felt her intake of breath when his fingers inched upward then closed over the top of one rounded breast. He could feel the taut nipple pressing against his palm and that knowledge sent waves of urgent desire into his loins. Each caress seemed to increase her need and he was more than willing to comply.

Slowly, deliberately, he toyed with the tiny silk-covered buttons holding her gown in place. He kissed each new inch of skin as she was exposed to his hungry eyes. Cade was finding it hard to exercise self-discipline. He glanced briefly at her flushed face before turning his attention lower. Her fingers fanned out across his chest as he loomed above her, eyes fixed on her. His finger dipped inside her bodice, teasing the hard nipple. It wasn't enough.

Cade peeled away the barrier. She made a small sound when his open mouth closed over the tip of her breast. He felt her hands on his head, holding him against her as she arched upward, toward him. Each time he flicked the tip of her nipple with his tongue, Barbara moaned and wildly ground her hips against his leg.

Placing his hand on her bared thigh, his fingertips barely brushed the sensitive inside, but he could already feel her responding. Her hands moved across his shoulders, massaging and molding.

Heat merged with pressure in his groin when she made brief, shy contact with his belt buckle. She explored the contours of his sex through his jeans. He found the silky edge of her panties and worked his fingers inside.

He lost all control then, guided by his incredible passion for this woman. He lifted his head and kissed her fiercely. His hand lingered at the waistband of her panties as he lay beside her on the bed. Slowly and deliberately, he teased her through the flimsy fabric for several minutes, reveling in the response it inspired. Barbara thrust her body toward him, all the while matching his demanding kiss. He could smell the faint scent of her perfume.

Cade lifted his head again, watching the stain of redness on her flushed face.

"You're embarrassing me."

He liked the husky, sexy tone of her voice and simply smiled down at her. "I don't see anything you have to be embarrassed about."

"Then why are you staring at me?"

"I'm not staring, I'm savoring," he said just before

lowering his mouth to capture one rosy nipple in his mouth. She responded instantly. Barbara's fingers played through his hair as he lovingly taunted each rounded peak in turn. Every now and again he heard her moan and replied by placing a kiss on her partly open mouth.

When he could no longer stand the pressure in his groin, Cade quickly removed her panties and his clothing. He pushed her back against the pillow, using his knee to wedge himself between her legs. He remained balanced above her, watching the expression on her face when his hips met hers.

He could tell almost immediately that she was as ready as he was. Cade had to school himself to move slowly. She wasn't helping him at all as she continued to grind her slender body against his.

"Slow down, Barbara, or this won't last more than about five seconds."

His mouth covered hers before she could respond, though he had a hunch she was beyond the point of lucid conversation. Carefully, he entered her. As he did, he heard her words of pleasure whispered warmly against his mouth.

With a single thrust, he gloried in being deep inside such sweet softness. When she wound her legs around him, Cade groaned and fervently kissed her neck and shoulders before returning to the warm, pliant recesses of her mouth. The rhythm of their lovemaking increased as his hands reached beneath her hips, bringing her even closer to him.

He felt her body convulse with wave after pleasurable wave. The sensation of having her body grip him brought Cade to a fast and furious release.

A long while later, Cade rolled to one side, cradling her against him. Barbara turned in his arms and placed a kiss on his chest. Her fingers toyed with his chest hair as she listened to his breathing.

"Are you awake?" he whispered in the darkness.

"Yes." She snuggled closer to him. "It's bad form to nod off."

"I have to something to tell you," Cade began slowly.

Barbara's brain went into overdrive. *What if he said he loved her? No. Not possible, too soon. But he sounded so serious.* "Go ahead."

Cade shifted away from her a little. She could see his silhouette, tell he was balanced up on one elbow. "I haven't been completely honest with you."

Every cell in her body went still. "How so?"

"I didn't bring you here just to protect you from Elvis," Cade said.

Okay, she thought. *Obviously, he was smitten with me in Charleston. That isn't bad. In fact, it's romantic. I can live with that.*

"I brought you here as bait."

Chapter Thirteen

"Talk to me?" Cade pleaded.

Barbara lingered in the doorway to the kitchen. She would never have come downstairs had she known he was still in the house. "The only thing I have to say to you is goodbye."

She refused to be swayed by his hurt expression. Besides, she was sure she was hurting more than he was. After all, it had been her brilliant idea to seduce him last night.

What was I thinking? She banished the self-recriminations from her mind. "I'm going to call Dalton."

She walked to the study, keenly aware that he wasn't far behind. Lifting the receiver, she dialed and waited for the connection. All the while, she was careful not to make eye contact with him. She wasn't going to give him the satisfaction of knowing just how deeply his deception had cut.

She was immediately put through to Dalton. "Seth called me first thing," he said.

"I'll take you up on that safe house now," Barbara told him without preamble.

"Well, er," Dalton said, hesitating.

"You can still protect me, right?" she pressed.

Before Dalton could respond, Cade touched one of the buttons on the phone, placing the call on speaker. "Is there a problem?" he asked.

"Not a problem," Dalton answered. "Of course I can arrange for a safe house. Can you bring her back?"

"No!" Barbara cried. Then in a more even tone, she asked, "Can't you send someone here?"

"I could," Dalton agreed. "It's probably best if we work out some way to do this safely and publicly."

"No way!" Cade thundered.

"We have to make sure Elvis knows where she is," Dalton reasoned.

"I thought the whole point of a safe house was to *keep* Elvis from knowing where I am," Barbara stated.

"The only thing we have on Elvis is the plate number Cade got last night," Dalton said. "The car was rented at the Helena airport under an alias with a fake ID."

"Can't they just stake out the rental agency and catch him when he returns the car?"

"Seth has the Montana State Police on that," Dalton assured her. "But Seth and I agreed that Elvis will probably ditch the car when he leaves Montana."

With me dead. Barbara blew out a frustrated breath. "Did you get a description or anything from the rental agency? Something better than Elvis?"

"Sorry," Dalton replied kindly. "No one remembered him and there weren't any prints on the contract."

Her shoulders slumped. "So basically, you have no idea who he is, right?"

"Right."

When Cade attempted to place a comforting hand on her shoulder, she brushed it away. "Tell me my options."

"We can fly you back to Charleston and put you in protective custody. Then it's just a case of waiting to get lucky."

"Waiting for what?"

"He's got to make another move," Dalton answered.

"You mean he gets to try to kill me again?" she asked incredulously.

"I'm sorry, Barbara. But unless we get a break, Elvis is going to have to come to us."

"You're sorry?" she parroted in her frustration. "I'm supposed to spend the foreseeable future waiting for Elvis to make his move?"

"Yes."

"When will that happen?" she demanded.

"We have no way of knowing," Dalton answered honestly. "It could be today, or it could be a month from now."

"Or a year," she sighed. "So you're telling me that no matter where I am, I'm a sitting duck."

"I wish I could do more," Dalton said.

"I can do more," Barbara announced.

"You aren't doing anything," Cade said with finality.

Ignoring him, she asked, "What if I stay here?"

"Barbara," Dalton warned, "what are you thinking?"

"I'm thinking that right now, Elvis knows where I am. He's bound to make another move sooner rather than later if I stay put."

"So?" Dalton asked.

"So when he does, Seth can arrest him and this will be over."

"I can arrest him, too," Dalton argued.

"Sure you can. In a week, a month or a year. I can't wait that long, Dalton. I've seen two men shot inside of two weeks. I've had a knife held to my throat. Seth has deputies swarming around here like picnic ants." Turning her head, she met and held Cade's gaze. "Besides, Landry brought me out here as bait. I might as well comply."

"Neither one of us thought Elvis would get to you so soon," Dalton insisted. "When we talked about this, we assumed it would take Elvis more time to find out where you'd gone."

"Hold on." She pushed the hair off her forehead. "You *knew* Landry brought me to his ranch to lure Elvis here?"

There was a brief silence, then the detective explained, "Yes. Landry and I thought that once you were safely tucked away in Montana, I could leak word of your general location to the press in a statement on the investigation of Dale's murder. We figured it was a controlled way to entice Elvis out into the open."

"Thanks a lot, Dalton." She disconnected the call before he could offer some lame apology. "It looks like you'll get your wish, Landry."

He gripped her shoulders. "I know I should've told you."

She stood rigid in his hold. "There's no excuse for what you did."

His eyes flashed. "I didn't plan on things happening they way they did. I didn't plan on falling in love with you."

Barbara forcefully shrugged away from him. "Don't make things worse, Landry. You don't love me. Love requires honesty and respect. You demonstrated neither when you took me to bed."

"Going to bed together was your idea," he reminded her. "And if you're honest with yourself, you'd remember that I tried to talk to you first. You weren't interested in listening."

She spun and faced him. "That doesn't excuse what you did. Nothing can."

He regarded her quietly. "I can appreciate the fact that you're angry now, but that doesn't change the way I feel. I'm sorry I screwed things up, Barbara. But I do love you.''

Afraid she might be swayed, Barbara quickly exited. She went into the living room and threw herself into her work.

He loves me.

How can he? He's been lying to me almost from the start.

Lord, she was confused. She couldn't forget how panicked she'd been when he'd gone after Elvis. Neither could she forget how perfect it had felt to make love with him. She sketched furiously. The bottom line was he had lied. She had compromised everything for a liar.

The pencil snapped in her hands. Anger made it easy for her to blame him. But that couldn't explain away her own behavior. What had possessed her to go to bed with him? It was stupid. It was unethical.

Barbara sighed and got another pencil out of the desk drawer. She didn't trust her emotions. Part of her wanted to get as far away from Cade Landry as possible. Another part wanted to forgive him. Never, ever, had she felt so off balance about a man. His admission of love wasn't helping, either. What if he really did love her? Worse yet, what if all the turmoil she was feeling was love? Her mind was spinning.

''I BROUGHT YOU some dinner,'' Cade said as he placed a tray on the table next to her sketches.

"Thank you," she replied stiffly, her eyes fixed on the computer screen. "You can leave it there."

"Am I dismissed?" he asked.

Turning in the chair, she scanned his face. Fatigue rimmed his eyes and caused tiny lines near his mouth. "I'm trying to finish the presentation."

"Where's Olivia?"

"I called her and told her not to come today. How was the funeral?"

He shrugged. "Hard."

Cade reached up and loosened his tie. Barbara told herself she didn't care that he looked handsome and haunted all at once. It wasn't her concern.

"You look beat," she said.

"I feel beat." Cade sat down and started to look through her sketches. "These are very good."

His compliment chipped away at her protective shell. Tension stretched between them like a taut wire. "Did Jessica handle it okay?"

He pressed the heels of his hands against his eyes. "She was upset, but my in-laws were there, so she was surrounded by people who love her."

"That's good."

"She asked about you," Cade said.

"What did you tell her?"

He offered a weak smile. "I explained that you have a maniacal Elvis stalking you, so you couldn't make the funeral."

She battled the urge to grin at the horrible absurdity

that was the truth. "You did make sure that she'll stay in Helena until..." Her voice trailed off.

"I told my in-laws what was happening. They'll keep a close watch on her."

"Good."

"I met someone at the funeral today who might interest you."

"Who?"

"Mrs. Carl Hilton."

Barbara blinked. "Did she say anything?"

He shook his head. "Not a word. I only know it was her because she signed the register at the church."

"Why was she at Dale's funeral?" Barbara wondered aloud.

"She must have known Dale when their spouses were working together," he suggested.

Barbara's mind began to whirl. "I've got an idea."

She turned back to the computer and worked her way into a genealogy board on the Internet. Cade dragged a chair over and sat close. Too close, but she didn't dare admit that to him or to herself.

"What are you doing?"

"Taking a back door into the Social Security mortality files," she explained. Cade thumbed through her demographic charts while she navigated the information superhighway. After a few missed turns, she finally found what she was after. "Well, well. Look at this."

Cade leaned forward, and in doing so, his arm

brushed hers. The contact sent a jolt through her. Obviously, her body hadn't yet realized that Cade was the enemy. She felt a tingling in the pit of her stomach when his breath spilled over her cheek. His face was just inches from hers. It would have been easy to turn and find his mouth. Easy but pointless, she reminded herself. She was already tied in knots; she wasn't about to make it worse.

"Carl Hilton and Mary Breck died on the same day," Cade said as he read the screen. "That's one hell of a coincidence."

"Do you honestly believe that?" Barbara queried.

"No. I'll call Seth."

"Let me log off first."

As soon as Barbara was off the computer, Cade called his cousin and explained what they'd discovered.

"He'll see what he can find and call us back," Cade said. "You should eat something. Mrs. Granger said you skipped breakfast and lunch."

Barbara eyed the tuna sandwich. "So I did. You aren't worth starving myself to death."

She was sorry she'd made the remark when she saw the pain on his face. "I can only apologize so many times," he offered.

"You're right," Barbara relented.

Cade looked hopeful. "Does this mean that you're willing to give me a second chance?"

Sadness welled inside her. "There wasn't even a

first chance, Cade. I shouldn't have turned to you last night. I can only tell you that I was scared and—"

"You can tell yourself that if it makes you feel better," Cade inserted.

"I-it's the truth!"

"No, I felt the truth when you flew into my arms out on the lawn. I felt it again when we made love."

"I was upset," she insisted stubbornly.

"If that's what you want to think, go ahead." Cade stood and went back to examine her work. "I did a lousy thing by not telling you everything."

"Very true."

"But you're the one lying now, Barbara. You can sit there and tell me last night was just a diversion for you, but I know better."

"You don't know anything."

He held her gaze. "I know you didn't chuck your principles for a quick roll in the hay."

"How crass."

"Maybe," he conceded. "But I'd bet the ranch that I'm right. You keep telling yourself that it was just a physical release, but I'll know better."

"Stop trying to analyze my motives," Barbara demanded. "You don't know me."

"Really?" he asked, his brow arched. "I know that beneath all that professional polish, you're a passionate woman. And a scared one."

"Can you blame me? Elvis—"

"Last night wasn't about Elvis, either. You're

scared of being in love. Scared it might interfere with your neat little life.''

"You're delusional," she countered.

"Whatever," he sighed. "I love you, Barbara. I know you don't want to believe that, but it's true.''

"How can you think you love me?" she asked. "Love takes time, nurturing.''

"Bull. Love doesn't have rules or absolutes.''

"Like you're an expert," she tossed out hotly. "You're divorced.''

"At least I was willing to take a chance," Cade fired back. "I'm still willing. Don't you think I know that you hate it here in Montana?''

"I never said that.''

"You didn't have to," he said sadly. "I know your life is in Charleston and mine is here. That didn't stop me from recognizing the truth.''

"The truth is that you're everything I *never* wanted in a man.''

"I know that, too," Cade acknowledged softly. "I knew all that, but it didn't stop me. That's another thing about love, Barbara. It isn't a choice. It just happens.''

The shrill sound of the phone saved her from listening to any more of Cade's definition of love. She didn't want to hear any more. It hurt too much.

She pretended to go back to her work on the presentation while Cade spoke on the phone. A few minutes into the call, she realized he was speaking to

Seth. Maybe they had found Elvis. Then this would be over.

This, she realized, included Cade. Knowing that should have made her happy. It didn't.

"Seth got ahold of the death certificates for Mary Breck and Carl Hilton," Cade explained when he was off the phone.

"And?"

His smile was slow. "They were together when they died."

"Together?"

"Uh-huh," Cade affirmed. "Seth managed to get copies of the notes from the state police. Mary and Carl were on their way home from the theater when Carl suffered a massive coronary. By the time a deputy got to the scene, Mary was near death, as well. She didn't last out the night."

"Joint heart attacks?" Barbara scoffed. "Didn't that raise any red flags?"

"Apparently not. But it sure has hoisted my colors," Cade quipped. "First thing in the morning, I think I should pay a visit to the widow Hilton."

"I'm coming, too," Barbara announced. Before he could object, she raised her hand. "I can't stay cooped up in this house. I'm bait, remember?"

Chapter Fourteen

"What is this?" she asked when he placed the cold steel in her hand.

"A gun," Cade answered. "Ever fire one before?"

"No," she said as she thrust it back in his direction. "And I'm not going to. I hate guns."

"So do I," he agreed as he positioned the butt of the weapon in her palm. "Grip it with both hands," he instructed as he wrapped his arms around her.

"I don't want to," Barbara insisted. She also didn't want to feel the hard outline of his body pressed against her back.

"If you're going to leave this house, you're taking protection."

"Even if I recognize Elvis," Barbara reasoned, "I doubt I could point a gun at him and shoot."

"Then just humor me," Cade said as he forced her to extend her arms. "Don't lock your elbows. Keep the barrel level and aim for one of those cans."

"You want me to fire this thing?" she asked, mortified.

"That's the idea. Now, aim and squeeze the trigger."

She did, and the recoil pushed her against him. The smell of smoke filled her nostrils as the feel of muscle teased her other senses.

"You're a natural," Cade said with appreciation.

Barbara looked up and was astonished to see that she had knocked one of the tin cans off the wooden post. "I hit it?"

His whole body moved when he chuckled against her ear. "Dead on. Weren't you watching?"

"I had my eyes closed," she admitted.

"Try it again," Cade said as he stepped back.

Barbara took a breath, aimed the weapon and pulled the trigger. Without Cade to brace her, she stumbled back as she again smelled and tasted smoke. This time when she looked up, the five remaining cans mocked her. "So much for being a natural."

"I want you to keep this with you at all times."

Grudgingly, she turned and lifted her face to his. "Does it come in any other colors? I rarely accessorize in silver tones."

Cade reached around and gave her fanny a playful swat. "This is serious, Barbara."

She moved her hand in an arc. "That's why there are deputies all over the place. If Elvis shows up, I'm counting on one of them."

His expression darkened. "The deputies will follow us to Mrs. Hilton's house. But that doesn't mean you should relax."

She frowned. "Relaxation isn't part of my vocabulary right now. What if Mrs. Hilton won't talk to us?"

Cade stroked his chin pensively. "We'll have to beg."

"I have a better plan," Barbara suggested.

Cade rolled his eyes. "Do you always have a plan?"

She nodded. "Usually. C'mon, I need to make a phone call before we leave."

Barbara took the copy of her rental receipt out of her purse and punched in a number.

"'Lo?"

"Jeff?" she asked in her sweetest voice.

"Yes?"

"This is Barbara Prather," she purred to Cade's great amusement. "I was in a few days ago. You helped me with my car."

"Yes, ma'am?"

"I was in last night," she began. "I was sorry I missed you, by the way."

"Yes, ma'am," Jeff said in a voice one octave higher than normal. "Uh, me, too."

"The silliest thing happened," she said. "I didn't check my mail until I was back home and there seems to have been some sort of mix-up."

She could hear Jeff gulp. "I'm usually very careful."

"I know you are," Barbara said. "I'm sure it wasn't your fault. But I have mail for box 007."

"I'm sorry, Miss Prather."

"It's no big deal, but I'm expecting a very important letter. Would you mind checking to see if my mail was put in box 007 by mistake?"

"It wasn't," Jeff said without hesitation.

"Are you sure? This is really important to me."

"Very sure. Box 007 is empty."

"Well, I guess I should drop this mail off to you. I'm sure the owner will want it."

"She will," Jeff said. "I really appreciate you doing that, ma'am."

Bingo. Barbara was grinning when she finished the call. "I was right," she told Cade triumphantly.

"About what?"

"Well," Barbara reasoned. "If Dale was being blackmailed, he had to have a way to pay the blackmailer. It's only logical that he was using the post-office box to make the payments."

"That would explain how someone could have picked up the letter you saw after he was killed."

"Jeff said mail was picked up by a woman. That woman has to be Mrs. Hilton."

Cade's brow furrowed. "I agree that your theory makes sense. But it still doesn't explain why she was blackmailing Dale."

She crossed her arms in front of her and stared at him. "My bet is that it has something to do with the deaths of Carl and Mary."

"You think Dale was able to cause two people to have heart attacks? That would be a neat trick."

Pursing her lips, Barbara thought for a minute, then went to the computer with Cade in tow. Again, she relied on the Internet for assistance.

"What's all this?" Cade asked as she continued to search.

Barbara glanced over her shoulder and said, "That is a list of suggested market buys for the cartel."

"Market buys?"

"Print and media outlets I think would provide the most cost-effective saturation for the campaign," she explained. "I'll tell you all about it during my presentation. Be quiet so I can concentrate." Barbara found a message board for crime junkies and began to scan topics. After disregarding the first hundred, she spotted something promising. "Nicotine poisoning."

"Dale didn't smoke," Cade said as he moved behind her to read the screen.

Shaking her head, Barbara pointed to the third paragraph of the article. "There are two cases here. One in 1940 and another in 1968. In the second instance, one sister killed another by lacing a drink with a high concentration of nicotine."

"But she got caught," Cade pointed out.

Barbara shut down the machine. "Call Seth and see if they did tox screens on Mary and Carl."

He got Seth on the line. The two spoke for a moment, then Cade said, "According to Seth, no toxicology was deemed necessary because of the age of the victims and the doctor's confirmation that both had died from heart failure.''

"Did the police find anything in the car?"

Cade asked the question, listened for a minute, then said, ''A makeup case, some costumes, Mary's purse and a thermos.''

Excitement tingled through her. ''The article said nicotine could be introduced by ingestion or through skin absorption. See if Seth can get his hands on the makeup and the thermos.''

Cade did as instructed, then ended the call. ''Seth is going to contact the state police to see if those items are still in their property room. But—'' his expression was almost apologetic ''—he thinks they would've returned everything to the next of kin as soon as the deaths were ruled a result of natural causes.''

"That's not good," Barbara opined. "But I think we have enough suspicious stuff to confront her."

"Talk to her," Cade corrected. "You could be right on the mark, but you could be wrong. All we have is supposition at this point."

Barbara patted his hand. "Don't be such a pessimist, Landry. If I'm right, we know who was blackmailing Dale and why." She put the gun into her purse. "Let's go calling."

One marked police car was in front of them, another behind as Cade drove the long distance from his ranch to Jasper. It surprised her that she didn't feel more frightened. Elvis could be anywhere. She sneaked a glance at Cade's strong profile. She noted the determined set of his jaw, the deep lines of concentration by his mouth.

"What are you thinking?" she asked.

"If Mrs. Hilton was blackmailing Dale, why would she have him shot? Isn't that like killing the proverbial goose?"

"Dale was behind on the payments before he died," Barbara reminded him. "Maybe Elvis was supposed to wound him, not kill him."

"Perhaps," Cade conceded. "Speaking of wounds, Thomas Shelton was treated and released last night."

"Good," Barbara said, relieved. "I feel terrible that he was shot because of me."

Cade shrugged. "He'll get over it. In fact," he continued with a little laugh, "he seems to think that because he was shot on my front porch, I now owe him the account."

Barbara cringed inwardly. "He may have a point."

Cade firmly shook his head. "I don't do business that way, Barbara. I'm going to give both of you a fair shake."

"How can you?" she asked. "If you give me the account, I'll never know if it was because of my work or the fact that we slept together."

"Unlike you, I can separate the two. I always have."

"How can you claim to be in love with me one minute and then swear that your supposed feelings won't get in the way of your decision?"

"The account is just advertising to me, Barbara,"

he answered as he briefly met her eyes. "It has nothing to do with my feelings for you."

"Then you have to be the most fair-minded, honorable man on the face of the earth."

He smiled. "I am. And I'm very glad you noticed."

Again her emotions fell into a tailspin. "You can't be too honorable," she said in an attempt to regain her emotional footing. "You lied to me."

She heard him suck in a breath and let it out. "For the last time, I'm sorry. Why don't you try to look at it from my perspective?"

"Which is?"

"My best friend had just been murdered. You were the only link to his killer. I thought if I kept you close, I'd be able to flush Elvis out. At the time, I had no idea my friend was a thief, nor did I think Elvis would be able to get to you on my ranch. That's what I'm really sorry about. I put you in danger."

Barbara's heart felt heavy. "Do you think it would've been any different if I'd stayed in Charleston? Obviously, Elvis is determined. I'm sure he would've found me no matter where I was."

Slowly, Cade's hand moved over to cover her knee. Giving it a gentle squeeze, he said, "Thanks for trying, but we both know you'd have been safer in protective custody."

"Really?" Barbara argued. "No one but Tracey and Dalton knew I was here. So how *did* Elvis find me?"

"My guess is that when he didn't find you in Charleston, he came here by chance."

"If Elvis was smart enough to use a fake driver's license to rent a car, he probably doesn't do anything by chance." Barbara pulled her cell phone from her purse and called Dalton.

"I'm glad you called back," the detective said. "You didn't give me a chance to apologize."

"No need," she assured him. "I need a favor."

"Anything," he said.

"Would you go to my office and see if there was anything that could have led Elvis out here?"

"The place is pretty much trashed," Dalton reminded her.

"Please do it," she asked. "Somehow Elvis found me and I'd like to know how." She gave him her cell-phone number and asked him to call back after the search. "That's another thing," she said to Cade. "How did Elvis get my cell-phone number?"

"Directory?"

"I don't list the number," Barbara told him. "And I don't give it out."

"Someone did. What about your secretary?"

"No. Tracey takes a number, calls me, then I return the call."

"Caller ID?"

"I have the number blocked," she said.

"Where is the bill sent?" Cade asked.

"My condo. Dalton checked," she supplied, anticipating his question. "There were no signs that Elvis returned."

"I'll make it a point to ask Elvis," Cade sneered angrily. "Assuming he'll remember after I finish beating him to a pulp." Reluctantly, Cade removed his hand from her leg when he made the turn up an impressive driveway that led to a huge, Tudor-style home nestled in a manicured lot. "Mrs. Hilton lives mighty well," he commented as he turned off the ignition.

Cade waved to the two deputies parked at the end of the driveway before he ushered Barbara toward double front doors. He kept his hand at the small of her back. The soft fabric of her dress reminded him of the silk gown he'd peeled off her skin. Swallowing, he tried not to think about it. Hopefully, when this was all behind him, he'd have a chance to make things right with her.

A Hispanic woman in a uniform opened the door. "May I help you?"

"We're here to see Mrs. Hilton," Barbara said.

"Is she expecting you?" the maid inquired.

He felt Barbara's muscles tense beneath his fingers. "We're here regarding Dale Breck."

The maid gestured them inside and instructed them to wait in the foyer. It was an impressive, two-story area with marble floors, a water sculpture and a domed, stained-glass skylight.

"It smells like one of those candle shops," he whispered to Barbara.

She responded by pointing to vase after vase of freshly cut flowers. "Since I doubt roses are in bloom in Montana just yet, she must spend a fortune having these flown in."

Mrs. Hilton descended the winding staircase like a goddess strolling down from Mount Olympus. Cade didn't know much about clothes, but he knew enough to guess hers were custom-made by a designer. Diamonds sparkled at her ears just below her expertly coiffed gray hair. The tennis bracelet on her right wrist was large enough to fall into the gaudy category.

Peering at them with guarded green eyes, she offered her hand. Her heavy perfume battled with the rose blossoms. "Lucinda said you were here regarding Dale Breck?"

Cade nodded. "I'm Cade Landry. I saw you at the funeral yesterday."

Her cool expression never wavered. "Yes. I was sorry to hear of his death." She turned her attention to Barbara. "And you are?"

Barbara introduced herself. "May we sit for a minute?"

Mrs. Hilton turned in a whirl of pastel fabric. "I'll have Lucinda bring tea into the library."

The library was just that. Floor-to-ceiling shelves were filled with leather-bound volumes. "You must be an avid reader," he noted as he took a seat next to Barbara on a crushed-velvet settee.

"It passes the time," she acknowledged primly. "I used to teach English."

"Nice digs for a retired teacher," Cade remarked.

Mrs. Hilton poured tea from the silver service delivered by the maid. "Sugar?"

"No thanks."

She supplied them each with a cup and saucer, then pushed a plate of delicate miniature pastries within their reach. "I'm afraid I don't understand the reason for your visit, Mr. Landry."

"Blackmail," Barbara answered.

Mrs. Hilton's eyes flashed, but that was the extent of her outward reaction. "Miss Prather, I have no idea what you're talking about." Her smile was thin and forced.

Barbara placed her cup on the table and leaned forward. Cade was content to let her continue for now. This was one instance when Barbara's directness might be an asset.

"Dale Breck was murdered at my party," Barbara said.

"How terrible," Mrs. Hilton said without genuine emotion. "But I fail to see what that has to do with me."

"You were blackmailing Dale."

"Where did you ever get such an absurd notion?" the woman scoffed as she touched the diamond choker at her throat.

"Montana Rentals."

Direct hit, Cade thought as the woman's mask slipped a notch.

"Y-you still have me at a loss," Mrs. Hilton insisted. "You have come into my home and made these wild accusations, so you give me no alternative but to ask you to leave." She stood, clearly uneasy.

"In a minute," Barbara returned smoothly. "See, I did a little checking and found out your husband and Dale's wife died on the same day."

"It was an unexpected tragedy."

Cade watched as the two women locked gazes. "I think it was a well-planned murder."

Mrs. Hilton gave a nervous little laugh. "I don't know where you've been getting your information, Miss Prather, but an autopsy showed that my husband died of natural causes."

"Because the medical examiner didn't have any reason to suspect otherwise. But you did."

"Excuse me? This really has gone as far as I wish—"

"Sit down," Cade commanded softly.

Reluctantly, Mrs. Hilton did and Barbara continued. "You knew that your husband was having an affair with Mary Breck. So, when the two of them suddenly died, you must have put two and two together."

"I repeat, my husband died of a heart attack."

"Let's hope so, since the Jasper sheriff's office is looking into the case at my request."

"What?" Mrs. Hilton wailed. "You're bluffing."

He admired the fact that Barbara managed to keep her poker face. "Dale poisoned either the coffee or the makeup they found in the car. Even after all this time, I'm sure a good forensic scientist will find traces of the poison."

Mrs. Hilton relaxed, and the dead, snakelike smile slithered back into place. "Very interesting theory, Miss Prather, if you could prove it."

Cade figured that was as close to a confession as they would come. He glared across at the woman. "Eventually, we will. Until then, you'd better hope that nothing happens to Miss Prather."

"I don't—"

"The guy you hired to kill Dale thinks Barbara can identify him. If you're smart, you'll tell him to back off."

"I didn't hire anyone," Mrs. Hilton stated unwaveringly. "Now, I insist that you leave."

Cade stood slowly. "We're going, but this isn't the end. I'm going to have the sheriff look into your assets, Mrs. Hilton."

"Don't threaten me," she seethed.

"It's not a threat. I'll make sure you go down for blackmail and felony murder."

"Wait!" the woman cried out, clearly panicked.

Cade glowered down at her. "Yes?"

"Just for the sake of argument, let's say I have been financially dependent on Mr. Breck."

He chuckled. "Nice euphemism. You must have been a good teacher with your command of the English language."

"Hypothetically, let's say I suspected Mr. Breck of killing my husband and that tart."

"A hypothetical tart?" Barbara asked sweetly. The question earned her a vicious look from the older woman.

"What would you call a woman who steals your husband while you're putting in long days at a public school and longer nights tutoring misfits just to get by?" Mrs. Hilton walked over to the bookshelves and ran her hand along the spines. Her expression was trancelike. "I suspected, but Carl always denied it. I loved him and I was working hard to save my marriage when Carl died. First Mary took his heart and then Dale took his life. I was entitled to everything Dale gave me."

"We'd better call Seth," Cade suggested.

"Go ahead," Mrs. Hilton dared him. "You can't prove any of this and I'll deny I ever said a word."

"Deny away," Cade retorted. "I'm sure it won't take the authorities long to tie you to Dale's killer."

"You seem like a fairly intelligent man, Mr. Landry. All this—" she paused and looked around the impressive room "—is a result of Dale's generosity. I had every reason to want him alive."

"So you say," Barbara commented. "Let's call Seth."

"Make your call, Mr. Landry. I promise you, there is no evidence left. The police returned everything to me five years ago. I destroyed it all before I went to Dale's funeral. I'll claim everything Dale gave me was because I was his mistress. Neither one of you can prove otherwise."

"I'm willing to try," Cade assured her as he waited for Seth to answer.

"Sheriff Landry's office."

"It's Cade. I need to talk to Seth."

Myrtle's voice was shrill with excitement. "I was just going to call you. One of the deputies spotted Elvis's car at a motel on Highway 320. Seth's on his way there now."

Chapter Fifteen

"He's dead?" Barbara gasped when she saw the black body bag on the ground between two parked cars.

Seth nodded. "He drew on one of my men. My man didn't have a choice."

Cade draped an arm over her shoulder and pulled her against his side. "I can't say as I'm sorry. Any idea who he is?"

"No," Seth said before giving the okay for the body to be removed. "We'll run his prints as soon as we get him to the morgue. I'll bet he's in the system. We found an arsenal in his room. The kind of high-tech stuff a professional uses. Oh," he said as he reached into his shirt pocket and produced a minicassette recorder. "We found this, too."

As soon as Seth pressed the play button, Tracey's voice spilled from the machine. "...full pay?"

"That was the day after the break-in," Barbara said. "How did Elvis tape our conversation?"

"I spoke to Dalton a few minutes ago. They found

a transmitter under your secretary's keyboard drawer. He must have planted it when he trashed your office.''

Barbara shivered and leaned closer to Cade. ''He sure went to a lot of trouble. I hope Mrs. Hilton paid him well.''

Cade and Barbara went to Seth's office and told him all about their visit with Carl's widow. They explained the probable murder of Carl Hilton and Mary Breck, including the fact that Dale had been the mastermind. The subsequent blackmail seemed to bother Seth.

''Why would she have him killed?'' he asked.

''I think Elvis was just supposed to scare him,'' Barbara conjectured. ''I had grabbed ahold of Dale just as the shot was fired. Maybe that's why Elvis killed him instead of warning him.''

''But didn't you say you found evidence that Dale had caught up on his payments the day before he went to Charleston?'' Seth asked.

Barbara shrugged. ''Yes, but maybe Mrs. Hilton didn't pick the money up from the box at Montana Rentals. She probably didn't know that Dale had scraped together the money.''

She didn't like the fact that Seth was so fixated on details. She wanted to relish in the knowledge that she was no longer living under a death threat, not try to explain the actions of a blackmailer or a hired killer.

''I'll take Barbara back to the ranch,'' Cade said

as if he'd read her mind. "You can call if you have any more questions."

"I'll try to tie this up as soon as possible," Seth promised. "Will you stay at the Lazy L until I finish the investigation?"

Her heart stopped and seized at the question. Careful to keep her eyes averted, she said, "I'm going back to Charleston tomorrow."

"What about your presentation?" Cade asked almost frantically.

"I can have everything together for you in the morning. It won't take me more than about an hour. I'll leave in the afternoon."

Cade remained completely silent as they left the sheriff's office and returned to the ranch. Barbara wanted to speak several times, but she just couldn't find words to describe her own jumbled feelings. It was better this way, she decided. She would talk to him about the account and leave everything else alone.

"Great!" she heard Cade grumble when they arrived at the house and found both Jessica and Olivia waiting for them.

Barbara was alternately relieved and sorry.

"I told you to stay in Helena for the weekend," Cade admonished when Jessica greeted them at the front door.

She cast Barbara an unwelcome glare before pouting up at her father. "Grans promised me you'd explain why you haven't wanted me around lately. I couldn't wait to hear.''

"Mr. Landry?" Olivia began timidly.

"Yes?"

"A Mr. Shelton called you. He said he was returning to New York to recuperate and wants you to meet him at the cartel office in an hour."

"Daddy!" Jessica wailed.

Cade put his hands on Jessica's shoulders. "I owe this guy, Jess. You and I can talk as soon as I get back.''

"Can I go for a ride while you're out?"

Cade shook his head. "Wait until I get back. I don't want you anywhere near the barn. Got it?"

Jessica pursed her lips, then stormed up the stairs muttering something about hating life in general.

Cade's eyes locked on Barbara. "I want to talk to you, too."

Forcing a smile to her lips, she said, "We'll talk about the account."

"Not the account," he corrected in a low voice.

Barbara blushed, knowing full well Olivia could hear their conversation and draw the obvious conclusions. "Yes, the account, Cade. It's better this way."

He gripped her arm urgently. "For whom?"

Honesty. She answered, "For me."

Barbara went into the living room and put her purse on the desk. Hearing the thud, she remembered the gun. Not wanting any part of the weapon, she took it from her bag and put it in the top drawer of the desk.

"I've finished the sketches," she told Olivia. "I'm going to go upstairs for a bit. While I'm gone, would you scan them into the machine?"

"Of course," Olivia promised. "Is there anything else I can do for you?"

Barbara smiled weakly. "Nope. I just need to make a few calls and finish packing."

"I'll get right to work."

Barbara climbed the stairs with a heavy heart. It was amazing that she had been at the ranch for such a short time, yet the thought of leaving filled her with incredible sadness. Well, nothing a good cry wouldn't fix, she mused as she entered her bedroom.

Jessica was sitting in the middle of her bed.

"Can I help you?" Barbara asked.

Jessica watched her with cautious eyes. "Are you leaving?"

Barbara nodded. "Yes."

"Why?"

The question caught her off guard. She'd expected the surly girl to react with unbridled glee. "I live in Charleston."

"So?"

Barbara went to the closet and pulled out her suitcase. "When you finish something, you go home. That's how it works."

"My father doesn't want you to leave."

Hearing that put a lump the size of a golf ball in her throat. "He'll get over it."

"How come you don't love him?" Jessica pressed.

Sighing, Barbara sat down on the edge of the bed. "It isn't that simple."

"Don't talk in circles," Jessica implored. "Tell me the truth. I'm the one who'll have to see him walking around all gloomy and stuff after you bail."

"I have strong feelings for your father," Barbara hedged.

"Then how can you leave?"

Twirling her hair around her finger, Barbara tried to organize her conflicting thoughts. "Charleston is my home, Jessica. I've lived there my whole life."

"So you'll move here."

"I have a business."

"Which you and that snooty Olivia person have been doing here all week."

She suddenly hated teenage single-mindedness. "That was one project. I have other clients."

"I'm sure you're not the only advertising person in South Carolina," Jessica reasoned. "They could find someone else."

"I don't understand, Jessica. You haven't given me any reason to think you can tolerate me, so why are you trying to talk me into staying?"

The girl shrugged. "Because I love my dad and I want him to be happy. He told Grans that you make him happy."

"He's had a rough couple of weeks," Barbara explained. "In time, he'll get back to normal."

Jessica donned an expression serious beyond her years. "I don't think so."

"Trust me, Jessica. He'll be fine."

The girl got off the bed and went to the door. "I know my dad and I think you're wrong. I think what you're doing is flat-out mean and hateful."

"Jessica!" Barbara called, but the girl had already slammed out of the room.

So Cade had told his in-laws about his feelings for her. She wondered why. Surely he had to have known that they would tell Jessica. Damn him for involving his daughter in all this. Anger fueled her as she packed everything but the bare essentials. When she was finished, she went down to complete her work for the account.

She went into the living room and found Jessica bending over Olivia's briefcase. She held a file folder in her hand and seemed to be reading the contents.

"Put that back!" Barbara admonished. "Because of other things, I didn't tell your father that you went through my purse, but—"

"Back up," Jessica warned. "First off, I accidentally knocked the briefcase over when I was watching the computer scan the stuff. Secondly, I didn't go through your purse. Why would I?"

Barbara's eyes narrowed. "Don't lie to me. You have no business in Miss Miles's things."

"Miles?" Jessica repeated. "That isn't her name. At least it isn't the name on all this junk."

Barbara went to Jessica and yanked the folder out of her hands. She read the salutation on the report cover. "'Dear Mrs. Shelton.'"

"That's right," Olivia said.

Barbara turned, shoving Jessica behind her reflexively when she saw the gun pointed in their direction. There wasn't a trace of the timid person in the angry woman who stood before her.

"Thomas Shelton is my husband," Olivia said.

"If he's your husband, how come you've been working so hard to help me win the account?"

Olivia laughed coldly. "I'll let Thomas explain that to you."

Thomas Shelton stepped into the room, taking the gun from his wife. Even with one arm in a sling, Shelton seemed like a formidable opponent.

"Barbara?" Jessica whined softly. "What is all this?"

"Hush," she soothed, never taking her eyes off Shelton. "Just a misunderstanding. Stay calm."

"Yes, Miss Landry, stay calm," Shelton mocked. "This has nothing to do with you."

"What does it have to do with?" Barbara asked. "I can't believe you want the account this badly."

"Barbara, Barbara, Barbara," he taunted, shaking his head. "I'm not even an advertising rep. It was all a front. I'm surprised you haven't figured it out yet."

"Obviously not."

"I'll give you some clues," he said. "Olivia dear, get me some of Landry's whiskey while I educate Princess Prather."

"Why?" Barbara demanded, totally confused. "Why are you doing this if not for the account?"

Shelton sat on the sofa, casually lifted his feet and

rested them on her drawings. "Clue number one—red hair."

It made no sense. "So I have red hair. So do you."

Shelton smiled as his evil eyes narrowed to angry slits. "Don't get disrespectful, princess."

"Stop calling me that," she spit as her nerves began to fray.

"Clue number two—who called you princess?"

"My father," she answered. "Only my father."

"Tell me about him," Shelton said as he used the barrel of the gun to scratch his chin before training it back on Barbara.

"If you let Jessica go, I'll—"

"She stays," Shelton cut in as Olivia returned. He had his wife hold the gun as he downed the drink in one swallow. "Tell me about him."

"He was a businessman."

"A rich one," Shelton stated flatly.

"Yes. He was very successful."

"Did he love you?"

Barbara nodded. She could feel Jessica trembling as the absurd questioning continued. Slowly, so as not to alarm Shelton, she reached her hand behind her and clasped the girl's hand. She kept her gaze fixed on Shelton as she steered Jessica's hand toward the drawer with the gun.

"He loved me very much," Barbara said. *I have to get my hands on the gun. Then what?* her brain screamed. *A shoot-out in the middle of the living room?* God, she needed a plan.

"How did you know?"

Her fingertips touched the handle. "I—I knew because he told me."

"He would've done anything for you, right?"

With Jessica's help, she began to ease the drawer open. "I suppose so."

"I don't want supposition!" Shelton exploded. Barbara started at the harshness of his tone.

"Okay," she said in an attempt to soothe him. "Yes, he did anything I asked of him."

"That's clue number three," Shelton said.

Understanding hit her like a fist.

CADE PACED IN THE SMALL confines of the cartel office. Where the hell was Shelton? he wondered. He'd been waiting for the better part of an hour. He wanted to get back to the house. He needed time to try to convince Barbara to at least give him a chance to make things up to her.

Dialing the Mountainview Inn, he asked for Shelton. The operator said he had left two hours ago.

"So where is he?" Cade asked himself. Maybe he had a cell phone or a pager, Cade thought as he went to the file cabinet to see if Dale had made notes someplace.

He began flipping through the alphabetical file folders. He stopped at the one labeled Prather, Barbara. Lifting it out of the drawer, he looked inside. He'd expected a résumé, correspondence, maybe a memo. What he found instead made his blood run cold.

He was looking at a detailed report of Barbara's life. Her education, vacations, jobs, friends. It was all there. "Why did Dale have this?" he wondered aloud.

Worried, Cade picked up the phone and dialed the ranch. Barbara answered on the third ring.

"Hello?"

"It's me," he said, relieved to hear her voice.

"I know, darling."

Darling? "I was just wondering if you were still using the gift I gave you this morning?"

"It was so special that I put it away," she answered. "I'm sorry now that I didn't keep it closer to my heart. Um, I'm trying to finish the presentation. I'll have to talk to you later."

He held the phone for several seconds before he dashed from the office. The tires squealed as he tore out onto the road. He drove directly to Seth's office.

Breathless, he bounded up the steps and rushed inside. Seth was on the phone when Cade stormed in. "Something's wrong. We have to get out to the Lazy L."

Seth's face instantly mirrored his own concern. "Let's go."

Chapter Sixteen

"Well done," Shelton said as he nudged her back over to Jessica with the barrel of the gun.

Barbara knew it was imperative to keep Shelton talking until Cade could get to the ranch. "You're my brother?"

Shelton glowered at her from across the room. "Half brother. I'm the dirty little secret of the family."

"I don't understand."

"Because of you, our father dumped my mother. He told her that you'd made him choose between her and you."

"I was a child," Barbara reasoned.

"I wasn't even born yet," Shelton fired back. "My mother was pregnant when he left her high and dry."

"That doesn't sound like my father. He wouldn't have turned his back on his own son."

"My mother never told him. She was too proud to go crawling to him for help. Instead, she worked herself into an early grave to support us. And all that time, the two of you were living like royalty.''

''So what will killing me prove?''

Shelton grinned. ''My mother wouldn't beg, but she was smart enough to put his name on my birth certificate. With you dead, everything will go to me.''

''How will you spend it in prison?'' Barbara countered.

Shelton smiled. ''I won't go to prison. Everyone knows you've had a professional killer after you. All I have to do is hang back for a decent period of time, then I'll step forward and take what should have been mine in the first place.''

''They shot Elvis a few hours ago,'' Barbara told him, hoping to derail his plan.

''So what. There's no way they can connect me to Elvis. The authorities will just assume that Elvis had an accomplice. Especially after Olivia tells how a masked man came in and slaughtered both of you.''

Barbara heard Jessica whimper softly. ''How will Olivia explain her survival?''

''I was in the kitchen when I heard the commotion,'' Olivia supplied. ''When I heard the first shot, I hid until it was safe, then I called the cops.''

''They'll know you're lying when they talk to the temp agency. I'm sure you had to give them your real name.''

Shelton grinned. ''She isn't from the agency. We bugged your office before we trashed everything. I knew which agency your secretary called. It was a

simple matter of calling them back to cancel and
sending Olivia instead.''

He hadn't left many loose ends. ''How long have
you been planning this?''

''Since he died.''

''Our father?''

Shelton's eyes glistened with hatred. ''He knew
about me. He was told the week before he died, but
he didn't bother to change his will. That left me in
foster homes. Can you imagine that, Barbara? While
you were endowing scholarships, I was being shuffled
from place to place. Do you know what that does to
a kid?''

No, but she was getting a quick education. Shelton
wasn't just evil, he was unbalanced. She had to think
of a way to get Jessica to safety. She needed a plan
and quick. ''Would it be all right if we sat down?''
she asked politely.

Shelton seemed to consider it for a minute, then
nodded. ''Slowly, though.''

Barbara took Jessica by the hand and led her to the
chair. Just as the girl was about to sit, Barbara
grabbed the pile of demographic charts and threw
them toward Shelton. ''Run!'' she said, shoving Jessica while lunging at Shelton.

Using the heel of her hand, she managed to press
against the gunshot wound Shelton had suffered. He
yelped in pain, Barbara joining him when Olivia
yanked hard on her hair.

A shot rang out and all three of them went still.

Barbara looked up and saw Jessica holding the still-smoking gun. Olivia let go of her hair the same instant that Shelton pushed the barrel of his gun against her cheek.

"Tell her to put the gun down," Shelton seethed between tightly clenched teeth.

"Don't do it!" Barbara yelled. "Get out of here, Jessica."

"But my dad—"

"Put the gun down or I'll shoot," Shelton barked, punctuating the remark by hitting Barbara's jaw with the weapon.

Tears stung her eyes from the feel of the metal cracking against her face. She felt herself go limp when Jessica surrendered her gun to Olivia. Barbara was roughly shoved to her knees.

Blood began to seep through the dressing at Shelton's shoulder. When he caught sight of it, he leaned forward and hit Barbara in the mouth. The blow sent her sprawling.

Jessica let out a strangled scream as she dropped to the floor and began to cry. "I'm sorry."

Barbara did her best to muster a smile. "Don't worry," she whispered.

"Worry," Shelton grated as he came over and waved the gun between the two of them. "Jessica, since you were such a good girl giving Olivia the gun, I'll let you die first."

The teenager cried harder and Barbara felt a flash of white-hot anger. "Cade's on his way here!"

Shelton gave her an I-don't-believe-you glance. "Not possible. He'll wait for me because of last night." Shelton's expression grew impatient. "I was really pissed when I took the bullet intended for you. Then I thought, what the hell, who would ever suspect that I was involved?"

"I'm telling you," Barbara insisted as she tried to block Jessica, "Cade is coming."

"I was listening in. You didn't give him any reason to come racing back here."

"Ask your wife," Barbara instructed. "Ask her if she's ever heard me call Cade darling."

"Uh, I haven't," Olivia admitted. A spark of fear found its way into the woman's eyes. "What if she's telling the truth?"

"She's lying to stay alive," Shelton insisted, agitated. "Which—"

The sound of a car out front silenced him. As soon as his attention was diverted, Barbara grabbed the sobbing girl and held her. Shelton let out a string of vile curses.

"Get up!" he barked.

Barbara helped Jessica stand. "You're caught, Shelton," she warned. "Don't make it worse by—"

"Shut up!" He reached out and yanked Jessica away from Barbara. The girl cried as Shelton shoved her beneath his arm and held the gun to her head. "Watch her," he told his wife before he went to the door.

The gun Olivia held on her was trembling. Barbara

hoped that meant she wasn't quite as eager to commit murder as her husband.

"Back off!" she heard Shelton yell.

The pained sound of Cade calling his daughter's name was enough of a distraction. Barbara lunged at Olivia, grabbing the gun and backhanding the woman so she couldn't scream. Before Olivia could hit the ground, Barbara grabbed her and held the gun to her temple.

Dragging her along, she went up behind Shelton. She could just see Cade and Seth crouched behind the Bronco. Seth had his gun drawn. Cade was watching the scene with raw, tortured eyes.

"There's been a change in plans," Barbara said.

Shelton spun and his eyes widened when he saw that she now held his precious wife in the very way he was holding Jessica. "I'll kill her," he warned.

She met his gaze. "And I'll kill her."

Shelton looked like he would explode when Olivia said, "Please. Don't let her kill me."

Shelton gave Jessica a shove and the girl tumbled into Olivia, then Barbara. The three of them went down like dominoes as Shelton raced away. Barbara scrambled to her feet just as Cade and Seth reached them.

"Jess," Cade said, hugging his sobbing daughter, "are you okay?"

As Seth reached for Olivia, she made a grab for the gun Barbara had dropped in the fall. Shaking, the woman pointed it at them while she carefully backed out of the house.

"She won't get far," Seth assured them. "Everybody just stay put until she's in her car."

"You're bleeding," Cade said, reaching out and gently wiping the corner of Barbara's mouth.

Bravely, she smiled up at him. "Think it was something I said?"

Seth called in a description of Olivia's car before he ordered them to stay in the room while he checked the rest of the house for signs of Shelton. "He must have gone out the back," Seth surmised when he returned. Looking at Barbara, he said, "I'll put some ice on your face until the paramedics can get here."

"No paramedics," Barbara insisted, thanking him. "And I think I'd like the ice in a very strong drink."

While Cade calmed his daughter, Seth made Barbara an ice pack and a rather stiff drink. She felt herself wince when she placed the cold towel against her lips and jaw. Seth was seated across from her at the kitchen table, wearing a very Landry-like scowl. "What did you do to Shelton?"

Cade and Jessica joined them. It was apparent that the girl had washed her face. Barbara guessed it would take a lot more than water to wash away the terrible memories.

"She tried to kick his butt," Jessica answered, her voice tinged with genuine respect.

She felt Cade's eyes on her. "I'm afraid I'm not

very good at hand-to-hand combat. Even when my opponent only has one hand.''

''She threw things at him,'' Jess continued enthusiastically. ''Just so I could get away.''

''Which you didn't do,'' Barbara reminded the girl.

She shrugged. ''It wouldn't have been very nice of me to leave you alone.''

''It would've been a lot smarter,'' Barbara said. Glancing up at Cade, she added, ''Obviously, your father needs to have a little talk with you about avoiding dangerous situations.''

Jessica scoffed. ''You tried to help me. Besides, if I had run out like you told me, that Shelton guy probably would have just shot me in the back. You'll catch him, right, Seth?''

''You bet,'' he said. ''Until I do, how would you like to go out to the Lucky 7?''

Jessica's face brightened. ''Your family hires some majorly hunky hands.''

Cade chuckled. ''I see being a hostage hasn't affected your boy radar.''

''Man radar,'' Jessica corrected haughtily. ''Will it be safe over there?''

Cade nodded. ''I'm sure Shelton will be caught soon. But don't worry, there's no way he would look for you or Barbara at the Lucky 7.''

''Excuse me?'' Barbara said, adjusting the ice pack. ''I don't think it's such a good idea for me to be around Jessica.''

''Jess,'' the girl corrected.

Barbara smiled, knowing that she was now counted among the teenager's friends.

"If Shelton decides to come after me again, I don't want him to be able to get his hands on her again. Once was quite enough, thank you."

"We'll have to come up with a safe place for you, then," Cade said. "C'mon, Jess. Let's go up and put some things together for you to take to the Lucky 7."

Jess stood and gave Barbara a variation of a hug before following her father up the stairs.

"Let's go," Barbara said to Seth in a conspiratorial tone.

"Go?"

"I want you to get me out of here now. And I want your word that you won't let Cade know where I am."

"GET OFF, CADE," Seth said, bracing his forearm against Cade's throat. "I don't want to hurt you."

Since Seth was the one who was bent over the desk, Cade thought there was very little chance of that. "Where is she?"

"She's safe," Seth promised for the third time. "She doesn't want you to know where she is until Shelton is in custody."

"Too bad," Cade told him. "I don't want her out there alone."

"She isn't alone," Seth assured him. "I've got two deputies keeping an eye on her."

Cade felt like hitting something, and if Seth didn't

tell him what he wanted to know soon, Seth would be that something. "I have to be with her."

"That isn't what she wants," Seth counseled.

"She doesn't know what she wants," Cade breathed as he let Seth go.

"Seemed pretty sure of herself to me," Seth offered as he straightened his shirt.

Cade glared at his cousin. "Being hardheaded isn't the same thing. It's been hours and you haven't found Olivia or Shelton."

Seth shrugged. "We found Olivia's car abandoned out by the Wickwire place. I figure they changed cars and headed west. They're probably halfway to Idaho by now."

Cade shook his head. "Jess said Shelton was determined to see Barbara dead. He's been planning this for years. I doubt he's given up."

"Maybe," Seth said. "But she seemed pretty clear about you. She doesn't want you anywhere around."

Cade opened and closed his fists. "I didn't handle her right."

Seth laughed. "Cade, my man, don't you know you can't *handle* a woman?"

Cade blew out a breath. "This one is different."

"Really?"

Cade ignored Seth's teasing tone. "I'm in love with her."

"Tell me something I don't know," Seth joked.

"You've got to tell me," Cade pleaded. "Where is she?"

"I gave my word," Seth said.

But Cade was looking in his eyes when he said it. Slowly, he began to grin. "Where are your deputies tonight?"

"Out on the road. Except for two of them. They're on special assignment up in Hillsboro. A place called the Manor Motel."

"I owe you," Cade told his cousin.

"Big time," Seth called. "I'll collect someday, too."

Cade drove northwest, reaching the Manor Motel just at dusk. Parking in the lot, he easily spotted the two deputies sitting outside one of the rooms. He was on a first-name basis with both men.

He called out to them as he approached but neither moved. Alarms went off in his head and he began to run. When he checked the men, he found them both out cold. Cade reared back and kicked in the door to the room.

It was empty.

Chapter Seventeen

Tearing through the room, Cade tried to find something that might help him discover where Shelton had taken her. His body filled with rage and fear when he saw spots of blood on the carpet by the bathroom. Shelton and Olivia had somehow managed to drug the deputies. He was sure a check of the cups he'd seen by their chairs would prove that theory. "But where would they take Barbara?" he asked himself, hoping that hearing his own voice might help him.

Finding nothing useful in the room, Cade jogged over to the manager's office. He found a fat, balding man in a stained T-shirt sitting behind the desk, chewing on the nub of a cigar.

"There's a problem," he told the man.

"With what?"

Cade glared at him. "You've got two deputies unconscious in your parking lot and the woman they were guarding is gone."

The man shook his head. "Saw her on her way out. She said there wasn't no problem."

"Way out where?" Cade demanded.

"She got into a van with another woman."

"What kind of van?"

The man shrugged. "One of those minivans. Green one."

"When?"

"Maybe ten minutes ago."

"Which way did they go?"

"East."

"Call Sheriff Landry!" Cade barked. "And get help for those two men."

Cade ran back to his Bronco and peeled out of the motel lot, his heart pounding against his ribs. The woman had to be Olivia, which meant Barbara could be dead already.

He refused to think along those lines. Pushing the speedometer over one hundred, he passed two trucks and nearly collided with an oncoming car before he spotted a green minivan up ahead.

Easing off the accelerator, he followed from a distance. He slowed his breathing, trying to stay calm. He didn't want to do anything to spook them.

When the minivan turned off on a logging road, Cade drove ahead about a hundred feet, then pulled the Bronco over to the shoulder and parked. Staying just inside the trees, he slapped at branches to keep the taillights of the minivan in sight. It stopped outside an old supply shack.

His gut wrenched when he watched Olivia pull Barbara from the vehicle by her hair. He'd never hit a woman, but he'd gladly make an exception for Olivia.

He waited until the two women were inside before he worked his way to the weathered building. Cautiously, he hoisted himself up to the ledge of a tiny, dingy window. He could hardly see through it, but he could easily hear Shelton's raised voice.

"Because of you, I'll have nothing!" Shelton ranted as he shoved Barbara into a chair.

A single bulb dangling from the ceiling illuminated the room. Fifty-gallon drums lined one wall. There was only one way in.

Reaching into the back of his waistband, Cade retrieved his gun and silently went toward the entrance. He sucked in one deep breath before kicking in the door.

The wood splintered. Olivia screamed. Shelton glared at him.

"Come to watch?" Shelton taunted, pointing his gun directly at Barbara's head.

He was glad he couldn't see Barbara's eyes. He needed to stay focused. "I came to kill you."

Shelton let out a derisive sound. "See, Landry, you don't get it. I don't care if I die."

"Thomas?" Olivia gasped.

He darted his wife a silencing look. "I went to a lot of trouble to get my hands on the money."

"I'll give you the money," Barbara implored.

Cade's jaw clenched when he was powerless to

stop Shelton from hitting Barbara with the butt of the gun. "I told you not to make a sound."

"Seems to me like the lady is willing to give you what you want," Cade commented.

"It shouldn't be hers to give," Shelton yelled. "I was his son. I should have inherited. It was my right."

"Will killing her get you the money?" Cade asked.

"He's right," Olivia urged. "We can make her get us the money and we can go away like we planned."

"Doesn't sound to me like your wife is in any great hurry to die."

"It's over!" Shelton screamed at Olivia. "It's ruined. All I can have now is the satisfaction of knowing she won't be alive to spend the money!"

Cade began to move forward.

"Don't do that!"

Cade continued his progress, careful to make sure his gun was aimed at Shelton's head. "What do you care?" he asked. "You've already told me that you aren't afraid to die. I'm just moving in for a better shot."

"Stay back!" Shelton cried, lifting the barrel of his gun so that now it was trained on Cade.

"No!" he heard Barbara cry.

She sprang out of the chair and head-butted Shelton into the wall. His gun went skittering across the floor as he landed hard, with Barbara on top of him.

Cade grabbed Shelton's gun and shoved his own in the back of his waistband before reaching down for Shelton. Gripping the man by the throat with his free hand, Cade forced Shelton to his feet. He was vaguely aware of Olivia begging and crying.

Shelton's face was red and his eyes began to bulge as Cade tightened his hold on the man who had terrorized his daughter and Barbara. He could feel the man's pulse begin to weaken beneath his fingers. Shelton's tongue came out as he gasped for what Cade hoped was his final breath.

Cade felt the gun being pulled from his jeans and he started to react when he heard the shot. He turned just in time to see Barbara fall to the floor.

Taking the gun away from Olivia was easy. She was in a hurry to see if Shelton was still breathing. Cade lifted Barbara into his arms and carried her to the minivan. Gently, he laid her on the back seat, pressing her hand to her side.

"You could've been killed," she whispered.

He shook his head. "Stay still. I'm going to get the keys and make sure Mr. and Mrs. Shelton are comfy while I get you to a hospital."

BARBARA'S ROOM LOOKED like a botanical garden. There were flowers, plants and balloons all over the place. "I think this is getting out of control," Cade said when he walked in carrying a stuffed bear holding a heart that said "Get Well" in bright red letters. "This is from Jess."

Barbara smiled. "That was sweet. How is she?"

"Great," Cade said as he leaned forward and placed a kiss on her forehead. "The judge denied bail to Shelton and Olivia. The D.A. thinks he can get Olivia to testify against Shelton. She's already admitted she went through your purse and provided Elvis with your cell-phone number. Even with cooperation, Olivia will still go to jail for a long time.''

"Good."

"The doctor says you can leave tomorrow." He felt a stab of pain when she averted her eyes. "You probably shouldn't fly yet. Not while you still have stitches."

"I know. I've decided to get a room at the Mountainview Inn. Room service and talk shows for a week. Hey, don't look so glum. The bullet didn't hit anything important."

"It hit you," he said quietly.

"Don't," Barbara said, touching his hand. "You didn't shoot me. Think of it as a really interesting story you can tell your grandchildren someday."

"Yeah," he sighed. "I can tell them that my friend and mentor was a murderer and a thief. That he was being blackmailed by one person and used by another."

"Used?"

He nodded. "Olivia says she and Shelton paid Dale ten thousand dollars to set you up. That night at the Rose Tattoo, you were the target, not Dale. That lets Mrs. Hilton off the hook as far as murder, but maybe they can get her for tax evasion or something."

"Good."

"They've also identified Elvis as Wayne M. Harringer. He has a criminal record that started in the womb. Society is no worse off now that he's dead.''

"At least I can stop calling him Elvis now," she said with a small chuckle. "Somehow it sounds silly to tell people Elvis was after me."

"Barbara?" He caught her chin and lifted her head.

"Cade, you already made it clear to me that your life is here in Montana and mine is in Charleston. That they were and will be separate.''

He frowned. "I made that statement when you were bleeding from a gunshot wound. I would've told you anything at that point just to keep you talking."

"Thank you again for saving my life."

Cade stood and raked his hands through his hair. "I don't want your thanks," he told her. "I want you."

"It isn't that easy," Barbara argued.

"Really?" he countered hotly. "You took a bullet meant for me."

"That was different."

"How?" he demanded, shoving his hands into his pockets.

"Olivia was going to shoot you."

He met her gaze. "Why didn't you let her?"

"I couldn't."

"Why?"

"Because I couldn't."

"Why?" Barbara didn't answer. "I'll tell you why. You're in love with me."

She looked up at him through her lashes. "I never said that."

"You don't have to," Cade said as he took her hands in his. "I'd love to hear it, but I'm willing to wait until you're ready to say it."

"But our lives—"

"I've been thinking about that. What if I spent three days a week in Charleston and you spent four days in Montana? I can fly us back and forth."

"How come you get more days than I do?"

He blew out a breath. "I've got a ranch to run."

"I have a business."

"Which, as of one week ago, includes the cartel account," he reminded her. "Since we're now your biggest client, surely you could devote one day a week to the cartel. Technically, that means you'd be working four days and I'd be working four days, so everything is even."

"I'm sorry, Cade. I can't agree."

He let his head fall forward. "Okay. It will take some time, but I can sell the ranch and move east if that's what it takes."

"That wouldn't do it, either."

He looked up. "You still won't forgive me?"

"That isn't what I said."

Cade tried to make sense of her comment and her smile. "I don't know what else to say."

"Think hard," she suggested.

He did and came up empty. "I've offered to commute and to move. What am I missing?"

"Your plan is flawed."

"And as usual, I suppose you have a better plan?"

"Of course. I always have a plan."

"Whatever it is, I agree."

Her smile brightened the room. "It's a very complicated plan."

"Okay."

"The way I see it," Barbara began as she took his hands in hers, "you'd be miserable in Charleston."

"I could learn to like it."

"You could not. I, on the other hand, have already learned to like Montana."

"You'd agree to move here?" he asked, not sure he had heard her correctly.

"Maybe. If you'd be willing to promise me semiannual trips to the ocean."

"What else do I have to do?"

"Think about it for a minute."

Cade kissed her on the lips. "Please, Barbara? I love you. I want you with me."

She laughed as he lavished her with kisses. "What are you doing?"

"Groveling," he admitted as he placed the last kiss on her open mouth.

"Your groveling is nice, but it isn't part of my plan."

"Tell me," he pleaded. "Aside from begging, groveling, promising trips to the ocean and telling you how much I want and love you, what else can I do?"

Her eyes searched his face. "Ask me to marry you."

Cade's chest nearly exploded. "Come again?"

She shrugged. "If I'm willing to move from Charleston to the wilds of Montana, the least you could do is make it legal."

He kissed her for a long time. "I didn't think you wanted to get married."

"I didn't," she admitted as her finger trailed along his jawline. "But I figured that if I was going to be madly in love with you, I should go all the way."

"What changed your mind?"

"You. When I saw you burst through that door."

He wiggled his eyebrows. "Impressed by my brute strength?"

"No. I was impressed by your passion. I still am."

"Passion, huh?" he teased as he brushed his mouth over hers. "So what you're really saying is that you only want me for my sexual prowess."

Barbara laughed as her arms encircled his neck, drawing him closer. "You are the master, Landry."

He pulled back so that their gazes met and held. "I love you, Barbara. I'm not sure what I would've done if you'd told me to take a flying leap."

She traced his lips with her fingertip. "I never even thought about doing that."

"Really?"

"Really," she promised. "My heart seems to be ruling my head."

"I'm glad," Cade said, then kissed her deeply. "That's how it's supposed to be."

Harlequin Intrigue is proud to present
THE LANDRY BROTHERS
a brand-new series from
ROSE TATTOO author Kelsey Roberts.

Turn the page for a peek at what's in store for
you in the first LANDRY BROTHERS book,
coming to you in October 1999.

HIS ONLY SON

THE LANDRY BROTHERS

*Only from Kelsey Roberts and
Harlequin Intrigue!*

Prologue

"I got here as soon as I could," Sam said. "What's the big emergency?"

Miles Johnson was wearing his lawyer face. That blank, unreadable expression he donned during negotiations. "Have a seat."

Sam didn't feel like sitting. Instead, he braced his hands on the back of the leather chair opposite Miles's mahogany desk. He checked his watch. "I've got to pick Kevin up from the sitter in twenty minutes. If this is about the Littlefield merger, I've—"

"It's about Kevin," Miles said in a soft, even tone.

Sam's heart skipped. He had feared this moment since the death of his wife eight months earlier. Five of his six brothers had warned him, tried to prepare him for this possibility.

Sam stepped forward and fell into the chair. "You found him? Kevin's biological father wants him back?"

Miles shook his head. "No. The investigator I hired

couldn't find anything listed on the birth certificate you provided.''

Rubbing the late-day stubble on his chin, Sam tried to decide if that was good news or bad. Bad, probably. Part of him was glad the guy was nowhere to be found. Still, he needed to find Kevin's birth father to get the waiver. According to Miles, it was the best way to proceed with the adoption.

"So now we do the posting, right?" Sam asked. "Tell me what the notices have to say and I'll get them into the newspapers by the end of the week."

Miles cleared his throat as he shuffled some papers on his desk. "There's a problem."

Sam's chest seized. "You found a blood relative? You told me that I could still go for the adoption even if you found someone with a biological link to Kevin. You said the courts would take into consideration the fact that Kevin's lived with me since he was four months old. I'm the only father the kid knows." Sam opened and closed his fists. "Kevin's finally adjusted to Lynn being gone. I'm not going to sit back and let some stranger with the right DNA yank him away from me."

Miles lifted one hand. "Calm down, Sam. As far as I can tell, Lynn didn't leave behind any living relatives. That much of her personal history has proven true."

"What do you mean, *that much?*"

Miles slid a piece of paper across the desk. "Lynn was born in Ohio. Her father was killed during a military training exercise before her birth. Her mother died of complications from influenza when Lynn was 17."

"I know all that," Sam said, sighing as he briefly scanned the report from the investigator. "The courts emancipated her instead of putting her into the system."

Miles shook his head. "Not according to Child Services in Ohio. Lynn was placed with a family in Canton."

"Canton?" Sam repeated, surprised that it didn't bother him more to discover that his wife may have lied. "Okay, so she had a foster family. You aren't suggesting that they have a legitimate claim for Kevin? Forget it."

"Nothing like that," Miles assured him. "But they did provide some interesting information. Sam, it isn't good."

He took in a deep breath, held it, then exhaled slowly. "So tell me."

"Do you know what endometriosis is?"

Sam shrugged. "Some sort of female thing."

Miles nodded. "It's a condition that causes painful scarring internally."

"She wasn't in pain when we were married," Sam said. "So what does this have to do with Kevin?"

"Because of her condition, Lynn had to have surgery when she was with the foster family."

"She had a scar," Sam remembered. "She said it was from an appendectomy."

"It was from an emergency hysterectomy."

Sam laughed without humor. "How can that be possible? She didn't have Kevin until she was thirty-one."

"No, Sam, she didn't have Kevin. She couldn't."

Sam's gut knotted as he leveled his gaze on his attorney. "There has to be a mistake."

"I verified this information with the hospital where the surgery was done. Lynn had a complete hysterectomy just before her eighteenth birthday."

"So what are you telling me?" Sam demanded.

"Lynn could not have given birth to Kevin."

Sam blinked as his mind raced. "Then who did?"

* * * * *

Don't miss the first LANDRY BROTHERS
story—#535 HIS ONLY SON—
coming to you in October 1999.
Only from Kelsey Roberts and
Harlequin Intrigue!

HARLEQUIN®
INTRIGUE®
AFTER DARK

This August 1999,
two of your very favorite
ongoing series come together
in one extra-special book!

2 stories in 1

Rebecca York's
"43 Light Street" series
meets Caroline Burnes's
"Fear Familiar"!

AFTER DARK—for the steamy side of
summer when sensuality and suspense get
trapped together! Are you in more danger
from the killer on your trail...or the sexy
man with whom you're holed up?

Don't miss Rebecca York
and Caroline Burnes
together in one volume.

2 stories for the price of 1!

Available wherever Harlequin books are sold.

HARLEQUIN®
Makes any time special ™

If you enjoyed what you just read,
then we've got an offer you can't resist!

Take 2 bestselling love stories FREE!

Plus get a FREE surprise gift!

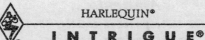
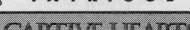

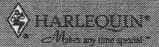

COMING NEXT MONTH

#525 AFTER DARK by Rebecca York and Caroline Burnes
43 Light Street and Fear Familiar—a special 2-in-1 Intrigue!
Two couples must hide from the day...and anything can happen after
dark....
Counterfeit Wife by Rebecca York—When a madman comes after
her, Marianne pretends to be Tony's wife—and can no longer deny
the desire burning between them....
Familiar Stranger by Caroline Burnes—When Molly's son is
kidnapped, she has no choice but to find her mystery lover—and tell
him of their son's existence....

#526 HIS TO PROTECT by Patricia Werner
Captive Hearts
In twenty-four hours, three women's lives were forever changed in a
hostage crisis. Now Tracy Meyer must put back the pieces and fight
to keep her stepdaughter, while sexy cop Matt Forrest moves in to
protect them from the hostage taker's revenge....

#527 ONE TEXAS NIGHT by Sylvie Kurtz
A Memory Away...
In the heat of a Texas night Melinda Amery found herself staring into
the double-barreled blue eyes of Lieutenant Grady Sloan. And he
wanted answers about the murder of her neighbor. Only, she didn't
have them—didn't have any. She had amnesia. But Grady was the
type of man who wouldn't let go until he got what he wanted. And
that included Melinda....

#528 MY LOVER'S SECRET by Jean Barrett
Only one man could protect Gillian Randolph from the madman who
stalked her: private investigator Cleveland McBride. Their sultry past
aside, Gillian trusted Cleve with her heart, but could she trust him with
her secret child...?

Look us up on-line at: http://www.romance.net